For Sarah.
Happy Bi...

Tom & Shirley

Dueling with the Devil

by Tom Huser

RoseDog Books
PITTSBURGH, PENNSYLVANIA 15238

The contents of this work including, but not limited to, the accuracy of events, people, and places depicted; opinions expressed; permission to use previously published materials included; and any advice given or actions advocated are solely the responsibility of the author, who assumes all liability for said work and indemnifies the publisher against any claims stemming from publication of the work.

All Rights Reserved
Copyright © 2017 by Tom Huser

No part of this book may be reproduced or transmitted, downloaded, distributed, reverse engineered, or stored in or introduced into any information storage and retrieval system, in any form or by any means, including photocopying and recording, whether electronic or mechanical, now known or hereinafter invented without permission in writing from the publisher.

Dueling with the Devil is a work of fiction.

RoseDog Books
585 Alpha Drive
Suite 103
Pittsburgh, PA 15238
Visit our website at www.rosedogbookstore.com

ISBN: 978-1-4809-7346-6
eISBN: 978-1-4809-7324-4

Chapter One

The Rev. Earl Thomas "Padre" Reynolds slid his golf clubs gently into the back of his 2001 GMC Yukon Denali. Padre bought and loved the Denali because he was able to remove all of the back seats and create an ample area for hauling food, clothing and other necessities to the good people he served in Ciudad Acuna, Mexico, a city of some 70,000 people just across the Rio Grande from Del Rio, Texas. He had enjoyed a good round of golf with his longtime friend Skeeter Davis. He took a long look at his scorecard. "Not too bad for an old guy," Padre said, and tucked the card into his shirt pocket. He stood motionless for a moment as he thought about the rest of his day. It was his day off, but days off seldom were really days off for this aging minister/missionary. There was often a hospital call to make, or the need to stop by the First Presbyterian Church to check with his good friend and colleague, Ramon Sanchez. But today really was going to be a day off. He didn't have any of those things on his plate today. As he began to muse about other so called days off, his thoughts turned to Ramon and their many joint efforts and good times on behalf of the poor people of Ciudad Acuna when he suddenly felt something pressing into his lower back. He lurched forward. Then he turned around and found himself staring into the menacing eyes of a young Hispanic man. The young man was holding a snubbed nosed pistol about waist high.

The young man said quietly, "You come with me." Padre looked around. There was an elegant black sedan parked on the far end of the parking lot. But there were no people in sight. The parking lot of the Del Rio Country Club had emptied as fast as it had filled early that morning. He was not surprised. No one wanted to play golf in the brutal Southwest Texas sun which reigned unmercifully every summer afternoon. After all, it was May.

Padre froze. He felt his heart begin to pound wildly. He perspired freely. He was frightened, more frightened than he had ever been in his life. He could have reached out and touched the young man, but his arms felt like lead, and his hands were trembling. The young Hispanic man had a demeanor he had never seen before, nor did he want ever to see it again. His piercing stare made cold chills run up and down Padre's spine. His mouth was dry. His breathing was short and shallow.

"Do I know you?" Padre asked.

"No, Padre, you don't know me, but I know you."

"But I don't understand. What do you want with me? If it's money, I'll gladly give you what I have on me. Or my Denali, is it the Denali you want? Here, take the keys." Padre reached in both pants pockets simultaneously and produced a smattering of bills held tightly in a tarnished money clip and his car keys. He held them out for the young man to take.

"I don't want your money, Padre, and, I sure as hell don't want that old rust bucket you call a Denali. I want you. Now, stop talking and listen carefully."

"I don't understand. What's this all about?"

"I said shut up! You padres always talk too much! I'll do the talking!"

Padre didn't need to be told again. He stood motionless and waited for the next command. It came quickly.

"I'm going to get in the back of your Denali. You're going to cover me with those blankets you have in there. Then you and I are going to take a little trip across the border with the help of your fast pass. When we are safely across the border, you're going to pull off on a quiet side street in Acuna. And, that's all you need to know for now. Oh yes, I nearly forgot one little detail. If you try anything funny, like trying to give me away or get away, you're going to hear a very loud noise as my bullet enters the back of your head. Don't think I'm worried about shooting you for fear of being caught. The man I work for doesn't accept failure, so I'm dead either way. Do you understand?"

Padre's heart was pounding. His chest was beginning to tighten. He swallowed hard. He stood frozen in time and space. He was speechless.

"I said, 'Do you understand?'" the young Hispanic man said, obviously getting agitated. "If you don't say something right now, I'm going to decide you're just too stupid to do what I tell you, and I'll have to shoot you here and now."

"I, I, I understand," Padre said, gasping for breath, his heart racing faster than ever.

"Bueno" the young man said, nodding his head up and down, flashing a brilliant smile. "It's nice to know that you are not as stupid as I thought you might be. It's also nice to know that I don't have to shoot you right here and now. It would make a nasty mess, and, besides, getaways can be a pain in the ass." With the last comment, the young man opened the Denali, got in and laid down on his back.

"Cover me with the blankets, and then put the golf clubs on top of me," he ordered. "Make it look like business as usual. Drive slowly, the way you always drive, don't break any laws, and don't do anything out of the ordinary. I want us to cross the border just the way you do on any given day when you cross."

Padre blinked, took a deep breath, and did as he was told. He slid in under the steering wheel and looked quickly down to the end of the parking lot. The black sedan he had seen earlier was gone. There was no one in sight. He started his engine, eased his shift lever into reverse and backed out carefully. He shifted into drive and turned right. He was on his way to the International Crossing. He saw a familiar car coming toward him. The driver was Betty Carson, his next door neighbor. She recognized his Denali and waved at him as she passed, a broad smile gracing her face. Padre waved and smiled back, just as he would have on any normal day. The most eventful drive of his life was going to be the most uneventful. He was determined to make it so. As he approached the crossing, he did what he always did; he held his fast pass up so the attending Mexican officer could see it. The officer hardly needed to see it. Padre had been making this same crossing almost daily for the past twenty one years.

"Hey, Padre!" the officer yelled out, simultaneously waving his left hand to motion Padre to proceed unimpeded into Mexico. Padre breathed an enormous sigh of relief. Then he remembered that his next assignment was to find a small, obscure street where he could pull over and get his next instructions. It was not hard to find such a street in Ciudad Acuna. He only needed to drive far enough to be well away from the crossing to avoid the appearance that he was making a sudden and unexpected turn. He looked ahead and saw an intersecting street that would lead him into a quiet neighborhood. There would be few, if any, people around outside in the early afternoon. Those who were not working and would be at home would be observing a siesta time. He drove until he came to a row of houses. There was no one in sight, and the pitifully small houses looked as if they had been abandoned. The whole area pulsated with an eerie silence, giving Padre the feeling that it was more like the middle of the night than the middle of the day. He picked a spot in the middle of a block, pulled over and stopped.

The bag of golf clubs rolled over to one side. The noise sounded like thunder to Padre. He tensed up even more, but he sat motionless, looking straight ahead. His unwelcome passenger began to stir from under the sea of blankets that had concealed his presence. He rose very slowly, and he looked around on all sides before he revealed enough of himself to be recognized as a passenger.

"Now listen carefully," Padre's new master said. "I want you to get out and come around to the back. Open it, bend over as though you were reaching for something; stop, then shake your head in disgust and crawl in here with me."

Padre stepped out carefully, walked around to the rear of the Denali and did exactly what he had been instructed to do. His fear escalated even more when he found himself lying next to his tormentor. He felt like he was lying next to a huge rattlesnake, knowing that any false movement on his part would produce an instant and deadly strike. He remained silent and as still as he could, with the exception of a horrible trembling that had taken over his entire body.

"Okay, amigo, you and I are going to change clothes. Now! Take off your shirt and pants and give them to me, here; take my shirt and pants and put them on. Again, Padre did as he was told. When the exchange was complete, the young Hispanic man tied Padre's hands in front of his body with a small rope, put a blindfold over his eyes and told him, "Lie face down. I'm going to cover you with the blankets. Stay very still, and don't make any noise. Do you understand?"

Padre was beginning to tremble even more, but he managed to say, weakly, "Yes, I understand." He lay down. He felt the unwelcome warmth of the blankets as they exacerbated his new blindness.

As soon as he had Padre tucked in, the young Hispanic man backed out of the Denali in the exact reversal of the way Padre had entered. He held his hand up over his face and rubbed his brow, hiding his identity, while he lowered the hatch on the Denali. He got in and started the engine, shifted the Denali into drive and made a U turn in the middle of the street. He went back to the main road that had brought the two men into Mexico. He turned right, and began driving down the road of entry deeper into the interior of Mexico.

Padre began to pray silently as he had never prayed before. He chuckled quietly to himself when he closed his eyes to pray. He was already blinded with two layers of darkness. What could he see anyway? He began praying, quietly enunciating his words under his breath, so that only he and God could hear. "Lord, I'm in deep trouble. Please help me. Lord, I'm so scared I'm afraid my fear is going to cloud my thinking. Please help me calm down and think clearly. Lord, I love you and trust you, and I put my life in your hands. In Jesus' name, I pray." The prayer helped, but the Denali hit a hole in the road, and Padre was shaken out of his reverie. He did notice, however, that something had changed. He was still scared, but he felt a strange new sense of peace. He felt, for the first time since this frightening intruder had come into his life, that he could now keep his wits about him, he realized that his attention to every sound, every smell and the very movement of the Denali, could make a difference in whether he lived or died.

Padre's captor began to drive faster. It suggested to Padre that they had left the city and were now out on the open road. The road itself had a different feel. It was smoother, suggesting that it might be a highway. Padre realized that he had not had much, if any, grasp of how much time had transpired since his ominous encounter with his new chauffeur. He had met him in the parking lot just after noon. He surmised that it must be one o'clock or even a little later. He felt a cold chill run up his spine when he realized that no one would even miss him until much later in the afternoon or even into the evening. By then he could be miles into Mexico.

The hum of the aging v-eight engine and the groans of an ancient drive train, together with the dull roar of the tires spinning over the pavement, set up a pattern of monotony. Padre thought to himself, "If I weren't so scared, I probably could get in a good nap right about now." He shifted his back one more time, trying to get comfortable in his undesirable position.

Padre's driver never made a sound. It made Padre even more nervous. It was as if the Denali was driving itself into oblivion, and no one even knew it was happening. About the time Padre remembered that he only had about a half tank of gas, the Denali slowed down. Padre felt the sway of the vehicle as it made a left turn. Padre ran the numbers in his head. "That's two rights and one left since we left the crossing; I need to remember that," he said to himself.

The surface of the road also changed. No longer were they riding on the luxurious surface of a paved highway, they were now on something much different, and rougher. Padre tuned his senses to the feel and the sound of the new surface. At first, he thought it was gravel. Then he decided it was caliche. "It's probably a ranch road," he muttered to himself. "Gravel is too expensive for ranch roads. This is just good old home grown caliche. We're on a ranch." His suspicion was confirmed when the Denali began to slow down again. This time, instead of a turn, there was a rapid thump, thump, thump. "A cattle guard," Padre surmised. Then he speculated that they were on their way to a ranch house, but where?

The Denali slowed down again, and it proceeded for some time at the reduced speed. Suddenly, there were shrill screams that sent a shock through Padre's nervous system. Then his memory served him well, reminding him that he had heard those cries before. He had heard them in Hawaii on a golf course. He was sure they were the same sounds. They were peacocks. Only peacocks could make those eerie noises. Wherever they were, they were on a ranch, south and east of Ciudad Acuna, where there were peacocks. From the frequency of the sounds, Padre surmised that there were lots of peacocks.

Slowly, but surely, the Denali eased to a stop. Padre's driver got out and slammed the door behind him. There was a ghastly moment of silence. Padre heard two men talking to one another in Spanish. Being fluent in Spanish himself was of little help when he couldn't hear what they were saying. He strained to hear. As they moved closer to the Denali, Padre could hear bits and pieces. He could hear enough to understand the he was the subject of their dialogue. He heard his name repeatedly. He heard his unwelcome companion on the trip tell the other man that there was no trouble at all. Everything went smoothly. No, he didn't try to get away. Yes, he was okay, except for being a little uncomfortable. And, yes, his Denali is a piece of shit.

Padre had hoped that it might be time in his adventure for him to have the blindfold removed. He was wrong. The two men opened the back of the Denali, looked at him for a moment, and began removing the blankets. They pulled him out feet first. They let him sit on the end of the bed for a moment to make sure his legs were working properly. When they were satisfied that he was stable, they lifted him out by the arms and stood him up behind the Denali.

"I need to pee," Padre said.

"Go ahead," the new man said and began laughing.

"I don't want to pee on myself," Padre said.

"Well, amigo, if you had two choices, one to pee on yourself or the other to die right now, which would you take?" The new man said, still laughing. Padre stood silently.

"Is he deaf?" The new man asked, laughing even more.

"No, he's not deaf, just a little bit stupid. Sometimes, it takes him a while to decide," Padre's driver explained.

"Well, he better decide pretty soon," the new man said. "Unless he's decided he'd rather die, then it won't matter. Because dead men don't need to pee." He wasn't laughing now, and his face took on the appearance of chiseled granite.

Padre stood mute.

Padre's driver moved to Padre. He untied his hands, and said, "Okay, Padre, let's see what you got."

Padre obliged him, but only out of his dire necessity.

"Aw, shit! Ain't that pitiful?" Padre's driver said, staring at Padre's penis. "Well, hell, I guess it doesn't matter how little it is, as long as it works."

Padre was paralyzed,

"Damn, don't just stand there, Padre. This is your big opportunity, opportunity grande! Let it fly, before we lose our patience with you!" his chauffeur said. Padre never had to go so badly, but it took all his will power to begin a stream, but he did.

"Bueno!" The driver cried. "Now that you've had a potty break, maybe we can get on about our business."

"Why'd you do that?" The new man asked. "I was hoping he'd decide to die. I wanted to shoot him," feigning disappointment.

"I'm sure you would, but he's no good to us dead. Besides, then we'd have to go get the front end loader and haul his poor dead ass off to the canyon and dump him. It's just too damn hot to go to all that trouble."

"Okay, Diego, you win this time." The new man was still chuckling.

Padre was trembling. His mouth was dry. His breathing was short and quick. He felt tightness in his chest and nausea in his stomach. He whispered to himself repeatedly, "The Lord is my shepherd, I shall not want…The Lord is my shepherd, I shall not want…The Lord is my shepherd, I shall not want…"

Chapter Two

Diego tied Padre's hands again. The two men escorted him to his new quarters. He stumbled more than once, but the two men held him firmly in their grasp. They told him when to step up and when to step down. Ironically, their care was strangely contradictory to their humiliating tactics. It sent a clear message to Padre that he obviously had some value to them. He didn't have a clue as to what it was, but he was glad for it. He knew that, without some future value to them, his life was over.

When the trio arrived at Padre's new home away from home, the new man, whom Padre now knew from listening to his two captors talk, was named Carlos, opened the door and led Padre into a room. Once inside, Carlos took a position in front of the door. Diego untied Padre and removed his blindfold. Padre was blinded by the sudden burst of light. He put his hands over his eyes and only gradually let them be exposed to the light. The light was, in fact, not all that bright, except by way of contrast to the total darkness Padre had known for the last hour or more. When he got more comfortable with the light, Padre dropped his hands to his side.

"You will stay here until Diablo Guero is ready to see you," Diego advised. "When he wants to see you, I will come for you. If you want to stay alive, do not try to escape. As you can see now, the windows are barred. Angel will be sitting just outside your door. The door will be locked, but if you should decide to open it and have some success, you will be shot immediately. Do not underestimate Angel. He has strict orders to watch you. This means that he is responsible for you. If you try to escape, he will kill you. If he fails, Diablo Guero will have him killed. Simple, Right? Do you understand?"

"I do," Padre said in quiet resignation.

"Bueno!" Diego said. "I will tell Angel. "Oh, and by the way, the reason we call him Angel is because he is known as the angel of death. As a matter of fact, he killed a man last night in Acuna. He told me he really enjoyed it. I will tell him that you are going to be a good padre, and he will not have to kill you. He may be a little disappointed, but he will understand."

Before leaving, Diego said, "Oh, yes, I forgot to tell you, I have all your personal effects, including your cell phone. You gave them to me when we changed clothes. I'll bring your clothes back to you when I have an opportunity to change into something nicer. Padre, you really should go clothes shopping. Your clothes don't do justice to a man of your standing in the community. They look like something out of a bad movie, and they are really very out of style. They're getting a little frayed around the edges. Even some new out of style clothes would look better. I'm really a little embarrassed to have kidnapped somebody who looks as bad as you do," he concluded and began laughing again.

Carlos began laughing all over again. "Si, amigo, they look like shit, really bad, old shit!"

When they had had their fun for the time being, Diego and Carlos turned and walked out the door. They closed it behind them, and Padre heard the dead bolt lock close. He heard the two men laughing as they walked down the hall.

Chapter Three

"Come on," Diego said to Carlos, as they walked briskly down the hall. "If we're going to find a birthday present for Diablo Guero before supper, we're going to have to get with it." Carlos suddenly found a new gear, and the two men quickly made their way to a large black sedan, the same one Padre had seen at the end of the parking lot at the Del Rio Country Club.

Diego and Carlos drove up and down the streets of Acuna for what seemed like forever to them. They surveyed every sidewalk and street corner, every parking lot and even drove around a small municipal park in the middle of town.

"I'm beginning to think the only women in Acuna are old or fat or old and fat," Diego said. But they pressed on in their search. When they were about to give up, they saw her. Actually, Carlos saw her first. He didn't say a word. He just pointed toward her and looked at Diego. They both nodded their approval simultaneously.

Diego, thrilled at what he saw, said, "Perfect! She is perfect!" And, she was accessible.

She was coming out of the HEB grocery store. She was carrying a small bag of groceries. She was about to walk across the large parking lot.

Diego and Carlos were mesmerized as they followed her every step. She was 5' 8" tall or so with long flowing black hair that glistened in the sun. Her face was roundish with dimples accenting her cheeks. She had on a tank top that was really no match for her large, full breasts. Her breasts bounced, challenging the boundaries of the tank top as she made her way like a ballerina across the parking lot. She wore short shorts. Her thighs were large, but not too large, just enough to give perfect symmetry to long muscular brown legs. Her flip flops accented her relaxed, carefree manner. Both men swallowed hard as they watched her every movement.

They moved their car ever so slowly through the asphalt canals of the parking lot. They made sure that they would arrive at her about the time she reached her car. There were ample cars in the parking lot, enough to give Diego and Carlos enough cover for their mission.

They made the final turn as she approached her car. They knew she was close because she shifted her grocery sack and began rifling through her purse for her car keys. All three converged at her car.

Diego was driving. He stopped. Carlos jumped out, ran to her side and said, "Do not make a sound! Come with me. Now! Or I will kill you!"

The young woman looked down and saw that Carlos was carrying a small pistol. He had it pointed at her heart. She froze.

Carlos grabbed her by the right arm, opened a rear door on the sedan and shoved her inside. He pushed her over as he came in after her. He put his gun in his belt, forced her down on her back on the seat and put duct tape over her mouth. He then sat her up and tied her hands with a small rope that he had been carrying in his pants pocket. When he added a blind fold, he was satisfied that she was ready to travel. He motioned with his left hand for Diego to go.

Diego drove out of the parking lot in the same leisurely way he had entered. People were parking cars, getting out, going in, coming back out, and no one was the wiser. It was just another busy afternoon at HEB.

Diego gathered speed as they drove to the ranch. It was all quiet in the big black sedan until Diego said, "Diablo Guero is going to be so pleased! We are bringing him the perfect gift for his birthday tomorrow."

When they arrived at the ranch, they pulled her out of the backseat. She kicked Carlos on the shin of his right leg. He retaliated by slapping her across her left cheek. She winced and began to cry.

Diego and Carlos took her inside and made their way down a long hall to a spare bedroom. They opened the door, all but dragged her inside and sat her down in a straight back chair. Carlos produced still more small rope and tied her to the chair. He then removed the blind fold and untied her hands. When he untied her hands, he noticed that she had an engagement ring accenting her left hand. He tapped Diego on the shoulder and pointed to the ring.

Diego took notice and smiled. "Well, now she is engaged to Diablo Guero." Both men had a good laugh.

Now that she was seated and secured, Diego stood in front of her and said, "Let me explain it to you this way. You now belong to us. If you want to live, you will do exactly what we tell you. You have two new jobs. The first and most important is to make our leader, Diablo Guero, very happy. It is not hard work. As a matter of fact, you can do it all in bed." Carlos laughed again.

"The second job, which you can do in your spare time, is to help in the kitchen. If you do what we tell you, and you do it well, you can be very happy here. If you don't do what we tell you, you will die. Do you understand?"

The young woman sat mute. Her eyes were flashing with anger. Diego slapped her again across the other cheek, and said, "If you understand, just nod your head up and down. Now, one more time, do you understand?" She was still for another moment, then, she began to nod up and down vigorously.

"Good! Very good! I really didn't want to kill you." Both men turned, walked out of the room and locked the door.

After what seemed longer than it actually was, Diego returned to Maria's room. He was carrying what looked to her like a complete wardrobe. He dumped a pile of clothes, shoes and a cosmetic bag on the bed. Without saying a word, he walked over to her and jerked off the duct tape in one motion. She cried out in pain. He was not affected at all.

"What is your name?" Diego asked abruptly.

"Maria Delgado," she answered.

"I don't need the last name. Here, you'll just be Maria. Now, listen carefully to me, Maria. I'm going to untie you. If you can behave yourself, I'll leave you untied. But, if you can't, I'll have to hurt you and leave you tied up all night. Do you understand?"

"I do," Maria said, uttering her first words since she checked out at HEB.

"Good. Good for you. Lupe will bring your supper in a little while. Don't do anything stupid like trying to escape. I have Jorge posted outside your door. He has orders to kill you on the spot, if you try to leave. He knows that, if he does not follow my orders, I will kill him. I will come for you in the morning. I want you clean, well dressed in the clothes I have brought you, not that trashy outfit you wore to HEB. I want you made up as you would for a special occasion with the cosmetics in the bag, and ready to make tomorrow the happiest birthday Diablo Guero ever had. Now, I'm going to ask you one more time. Do you understand everything I have told you?"

Maria bowed her head into her chest and said meekly, "I do."

"Get a good night's sleep, Maria. Tomorrow is going to be a very big day for you." Diego said, smiling as he walked out and locked the door behind him.

Chapter Four

Padre surveyed his new surroundings. His eyes turned to the one window in the room. Diego was right. There were bars, massive steel bars on the window, and the window was covered with a sheet of black plastic on the outside of the bars. He could also see that the windows had been nailed shut. The room was papered with a paper Padre hadn't seen since the 1970's. He speculated that the paper probably was the original paper. He was on an old ranch!

The only door other than the entry door led into a small bathroom. It had a different wall paper, but it too was from an earlier era. The bathroom did have the basics. There was a lavatory mounted on a small cabinet that looked like it had been bought at a garage sale. The Formica was beginning to delaminate on the corners. There was a mirror above with dark spots beginning to creep into the corners. The on and off knobs were cracked, and the faucet was beginning to crust over with years of hard water deposits. There was a toilet with a small cracked lid on the tank. The toilet obviously had leaked considerably over the years because there were water stains encroaching on the vinyl floor. There was a fiberglass shower with a plastic shower curtain. The curtain was adorned with butterflies in full flight. They more or less matched the aging wall paper.

Everything was old. But it was a bathroom. There were some plastic drinking cups on the cabinet top. The bed was an old double bed. It was made, and there were some old decorative pillows at the head of the bed. It was not the Sheraton, but it would do. It was also the least of Padre's current problems.

Padre looked around and wondered how long he would be there. He then remembered one of the guiding truisms of his life. When a little rattled or just distracted, he would ask himself "What is the best use of my time right now?" He decided that the best thing he could do for himself now, short of praying again, was to work on his breathing. He had been hardly breathing since his ordeal began. He was still feeling some tightness in his chest, and he had a terrible headache. Oxygen shortage, he mused. He began with deep breaths, filling his lungs to capacity. In a short time, he began to feel a little better. Even the headache began to subside.

He looked at his watch. It was his only personal possession that had not been confiscated. It read 5:15 p.m. He had been a prisoner for more than five hours. No one even knew he was missing, and it was unlikely that anyone would know for a long time. His wife, Midge, had gone to San Angelo to visit her sister. She was not due back until after lunch tomorrow. She would try to call him this evening, but his cell phone would be turned off. She'd leave a message, then another and another. She would be a little irritated, but she wouldn't be alarmed. He had a habit of turning off his cell phone on some occasions. He didn't leave it on when he was playing golf. He didn't want it to ring in the middle of his backswing. He didn't leave it on when he was having lunch with a friend, and especially if he was visiting with someone with whom he was doing counseling. He always turned it off when he was visiting with his friend Ramon Sanchez. Ramon, or, as the sign on the front lawn of the First Presbyterian Church read, The Rev. Ramon Sanchez, Pastor. Ramon was a busy man also. He would always tell his secretary to hold his calls when he was visiting with Padre. Padre thought it was the least he could do to return the favor. No, the cell phone that was an integral part of Padre's life would not be ringing. At this point in time, it really didn't make that much difference how many messages it recorded. He was not available.

Padre sat down on the edge of his bed. What next? What could he do now, if anything, to improve his current lot in life? He had decided that the best thing he could do for himself now was to lie down and get some rest. He was just lying back to take his position of rest when the door opened abruptly. It was Diego. Carlos was not with him, which suited Padre just fine.

"Padre, I brought your clothes. Get out of mine. Put yours on. By the way, I don't know whether you can play golf or not. With these clothes on, you might look like a golfer, and I'd say, from the smell of them, you'd smell like a golfer but beyond that, well, I just don't know." He laughed again with pride in his brilliant wit.

"What about my personal things?" Padre asked, reaching fruitlessly into every pocket.

"Oh those? Well, I think I'll just keep them for a while. You won't be needing them any time soon anyway."

When the two men had again swapped clothes, Diego got a wry grin on his face and said, "Adios, amigo," and turned quickly and left the room, closing and locking the door behind him.

"I won't need them," Padre said to himself, "What does that mean?" and he lay down on his bed.

Chapter Five

Padre closed his eyes. He might as well, he thought; he certainly wouldn't be missing anything of value in his room. At least, his eyes might get some rest. He might even be able to go to sleep, although he doubted it. In spite of his breathing exercises, he was still very tense. He wondered if it was possible to rest without relaxing. Probably not, he concluded.

He believed what Diego had told him. Trying to escape, even if it was possible, would likely only get him killed. Or, killed prematurely, he surmised. These men who were holding him prisoner obviously had a use for him. Otherwise, they would never have taken him, and, if it had been for his money or his Denali, they would have killed him long ago. No, it had to be something else. It was not hard for Padre to decide what that might be. He had lived on the border a long time. He had spent almost twenty two years now in border ministry. As he delighted in saying to any number of people, "I may have been born at night, but it wasn't last night." For many years, nothing changed much along the border. It was a very predictable set of circumstances. He came to minister to the poor people of Ciudad Acuna. There was no shortage of poor people. He had now served well into a second generation of the faithful in Acuna. They were good people. God fearing, gentle and faithful to their appointed tasks, they carried on a daily life in the midst of grinding poverty as their parents and grandparents before them had. They worked hard, complained little, and never let their thinking get clouded by unrealistic expectations. The exception to the rule was the young people. They had had all of the life of poverty they wanted, and they had never wanted it in the first place.

Padre recalled an eye opening experience he had with the young people one summer. It happened one evening when a mission work group from a Presbyterian church in Lake Jackson, Texas, had come down to do a variety of projects in one of the Colonias. Padre helped the group with their logistics, and he also served as a discussion group leader with the young people in their evening meetings. He loved working with the young people. They were so bright and so full of enthusiasm, eager to learn and full of penetrating questions. One evening, he looked them over for a moment, and then asked his question. "Where do you want to be ten years from now?" He was amazed at how quickly and decisively they had answered.

A good looking fifteen year old boy named Raul spoke for the group. With fire in his eyes, he said simply, "Dallas." The others nodded unanimously in assent. Padre didn't know whether the boy ever made it to Dallas or not, but he did know he was gone from Acuna. He was considered one of the "lucky ones," as they were known.

Padre often mused to himself as he walked the dusty streets of a Colonia and watched women come out and sweep the dirt (instead of grass) of their front yards. He thought, although only to himself, there's the beginning of a parable in here somewhere. I go home and mow my lawn. They just step outside and sweep theirs. What amazed Padre was that they swept with pride. He thought again, the pride of home ownership really knows no boundaries.

Padre was ashamed of himself for concluding on more than one occasion, I don't see why all the girls don't grow up to be prostitutes and all the boys don't grow up to be drug dealers. He was ashamed because he realized that he had just applied the prevailing standard of American materialism to the value of their lives. The truth, however, was that some of the girls had become prostitutes and some of the boys had become drug dealers, but not all of them.

The drug dealers were Padre's immediate concern. He was certain that these men who had kidnapped him and brought him into seclusion were part of a drug cartel. He also was just as certain of what they wanted of him. They wanted him to be a mule for them. They would take advantage of his years of faithful service and the trust he had earned on both sides of the border to have him transport a major delivery of their deadly contraband. It was not unusual for the drug dealers to kidnap someone's children, hold them hostage, and use their parents or a parent to bring drugs across the border. Padre had, however, been told that this plan, although it was attempted almost weekly, never worked. The Customs Border Protection officers were just too good at interrogating them. They always caved in under the scrutiny of the drug dogs and the relentless, rapid fire questioning of the officers.

Padre, however, would be different. He would sail through without incident on the wings of his fast pass. He would be met with a broad, appreciative smile and the wave of an arm. It would be no different from when he passed over every day he had crossed the border in the last nearly twenty two years. But what would keep him from trying to make an escape? He was puzzled. He didn't really think that Diego was ready to ride over with him the way they had crossed into Mexico, despite his bravado. He would not trust Padre not to give some silent signal to the officers on duty, and, even if he did, and they made it successfully, Padre and his Denali would soon be history. They would both likely die in an unfortunate fire in an abandoned building just inside Del Rio. No, Padre speculated that, if they had a plan, it was a mystery to him. He decided that he would just have to wait and see what developed. His one unwavering realization was, however, that he knew he was in the custody of men who were evil, cunning and brutal.

Padre turned his musings away from speculation to reflection. He began to think about his life to date.

He didn't bother to ask himself the question of how he came to wind up here today. He already knew the answer to that question. He knew his captors well enough to know that if they had wanted him, they would have found him. They would have worked out a plan to kidnap him. It was just that simple. They got what they wanted, even if people had to die along the way. They got their way no matter who stood in their way. Men, women, children; it made no difference to them. Padre had heard all the stories. He knew the tales of abduction, torture, murder and the spread of terror throughout the Rio Grande Valley. He had heard firsthand the frustrating stories of the CBP officers. He had witnessed the futility of their efforts. He knew he lived in a world of perceived tranquility that, in fact, was a simmering caldron of mayhem, waiting to boil over onto an innocent population at any time. He knew the fear it evoked in the people he loved and served.

It was not a matter of being in the wrong place at the wrong time. It was just a matter of being himself. It was a matter of being a minister and a missionary.

A fleeting thought passed through his mind. If he hadn't responded to God's call for him to the ministry, he would not be here. If he had not accepted the challenge to do border ministry, he would not be here. He didn't have to go into the ministry. He could have become a journalist. After all, Mr. Roberts, the owner/editor of The Wewoka Times Democrat, had told him that, if he would come back and work for him in his newspaper, he would pay his way through the School of Journalism at The University of Oklahoma. He could have had an exciting enough life as a reporter. He might have become an investigative reporter. He might even have had an opportunity to move into radio and television journalism. Sure, he could have done it. People might have been able to tune into Sixty Minutes on Sunday evenings and be mesmerized by one of his brilliant segments. But he didn't accept Mr. Roberts' offer. Oh, he really appreciated it, and he told Mr. Roberts he did, but he had this thing about being called into the ministry. It was obvious to him and everyone around that nothing short of embalming fluid was going to get the idea out of his head.

However, he surely didn't have to become a missionary. No, he didn't. He was a good preacher. No, actually, he was an excellent preacher. He could have easily become the pastor of a church, even a big, tall steeple church. That would have been really nice.

People would have hung on his every word. He would have been invited to be the speaker at large church gatherings all over the country. He would have been quoted widely. He would have been a political force in the church, a difference maker. Now, that would have been very special. He could have written a book, or several books and, people would have stood in line at Barnes and Noble to get his autograph on their copies. That would have been special.

Earl Reynolds could have done all of those things. But he wouldn't have been Earl Reynolds anymore. He would have been Earl pretending to be someone else. That just wouldn't work.

Chapter Six

Earl went to Austin College, in Sherman, Texas, one of the Presbyterian mating grounds of the Southwest and met Midge, the love of his life, and married her the summer before he began his theological studies at Austin Presbyterian Theological Seminary. He smiled as he remembered how they met.

"Hi, I'm Earl Reynolds," Earl said, looking into the dark brown eyes of the prettiest girl he had ever seen.

"Hi, I'm Margaret, Margaret Stephenson, but my friends call me Midge," she responded, flashing a beautiful smile that caused her dormant dimples to spring to life.

"Where are you from, Margaret? I mean Midge. Is it okay if I call you Midge?"

"I'd be glad for you to call me Midge. I'm from Mineral Wells. I believe that's what you asked, right?"

"Right, Earl said. "And, Mineral Wells is that in Texas?"

Midge looked at him with a wide eyes and a head that snapped back just a little. "You're not from Texas, are you?"

"No," Earl answered. "Oklahoma. Wewoka, Oklahoma."

"We what?"

"Wewoka. It's a small town about seventy miles southeast of Oklahoma City. Wewoka's an Indian word. It means "barking water.""

"You don't look much like an Indian," Midge said and giggled. "But, if you are, you're the first red headed Indian I ever saw."

"No, I'm not an Indian, not even close," Earl said, marveling at the effervescent personality that was bubbling up before him. "Would you like to dance?"

"Sure, I'd love to dance," Midge said, extending her hand.

Earl's heart skipped a beat. He took a deep breath. He was doing a miserable job not revealing that he thought he was just about the luckiest guy in the world at this very moment. He took Midge's hand in his firmly, but gently, and led her to the dance floor. As he took her in his arms, he looked deeply into those huge brown eyes. She responded with a broad smile.

It didn't take Earl long to realize that he was dancing with the best dancer of his life. She danced effortlessly, and she seemed to know Earl's next move before he did.

"You're a great dancer," Earl said, after they had danced two slow dances and a very fast jitter bug. You must have had some dance lessons along the way. Have you?"

"Yes, I have. I've had lots of dance lessons, and I have taught dancing too. I had my own dance studio when I was in high school. It made it possible for me to be here tonight. But you're not so bad yourself, Chief," Midge said and laughed out loud. "Oh, no, that's not right; you said you're not an Indian."

Earl loved every moment of their first encounter. He'd never met a girl so beautiful with such a quick wit. He realized that they had just met, and he was keenly aware that they were just freshmen in college, and he knew very well that this was freshman orientation, and he knew also that first impressions can be misleading, but, most of all, he knew he had just fallen in love, and he was not about to let her get away. He didn't. They were married the summer after they both graduated. And, they never looked back.

Padre shook his head in disbelief. He couldn't believe that he and Midge would celebrate their fortieth wedding anniversary in August. Their daughter Marilyn, who was just as pretty as her mother, would be thirty-seven in October. And, even more amazing, he had a grandson, Mike, who would be thirteen in January.

Padre's eyes welled up with tears as he thought about his family. Would he ever see his family again?

Padre had never been in a situation like he was in now. But he knew people who had. His years as a chaplain in the United States Air Force had put him in close contact with airmen who had been shot down in Viet Nam and become prisoners of the North Vietnamese. He had listened to their stories of brutality and terror again and again. But it had never occurred to him that he would also become a P.O.W. He was now a P.O.W. in the hands of a vicious drug cartel, who had a history of brutality and the spread of terror all along the border.

He thought about the many P.O.W.'s he had counseled in Viet Nam and later in rehabilitation facilities once he and they had returned to the United States. He tried to remember some of the commonalities of their experiences. There were several.

They talked of the shock of realizing that they were down in enemy territory. Padre could now relate to their feelings. He, too, was in enemy territory.

They talked of the terror they felt when they were captured. They described the near overwhelming fear they felt as they grasped the possibility that their next breath might be their last. Padre could relate to their feelings. He felt like the drug dealers had some use for him. He was not likely to die before they implemented their plan for him. But, after he was no longer useful to them, he felt a queasy certainty that they would dispose of him immediately.

They talked of brutality and torture. Padre had been spared these, at least up to this point. But he knew the terror that comes from intense and constant intimidation. He could only hope and pray that there would be no physical brutality and torture.

They also talked of their two most important sources of strength: faith and family. Padre certainly understood. His faith was strong. He could only hope it was strong enough, and he could not have loved his family more, and he was just as confident in their love for him.

Padre's thoughts again turned to Midge. He began to cry. He couldn't bear the thought of not seeing her again. But, what about her? What would happen to her if he didn't make it? He and she had talked from time to time about what the other would do in the event of the death of one of them. But their conversations were always focused on the distant future.

Padre said to himself, "Midge will be all right. It will be terribly hard for her, but she's tough, and her faith and her family will carry her through. She'll survive and move forward with her life. She'll be okay financially. Our home is paid for, and we don't owe anyone anything. I have a nice life insurance policy that we've been paying on a long time. She'll have my pension and half of my social security and enough income from our portfolio with Merrill Lynch to live a comfortable life. She won't be rich, but she won't want for anything important either. Besides, she's still the beautiful and witty woman I fell in love with at freshman orientation. Even more than that, she's a good person through and through. And, some lucky guy is going to discover her and fall in love with her just like I did. Yep, she'll be okay."

He breathed an awkward sigh of relief. Then it dawned on him that he had told people on many occasions, "It doesn't matter whether it's your wife, your kids or grand kids, or your church or your community or your country. Your first question is always whether or not they're going to be alright."

He felt like his only child, Marilyn, would be okay, too. She had never had to face the loss of a parent. But he just felt like she could handle it like she handled everything else in her life. She was a lot like her mother. She was strong and very deter-mined to make things work out well. But, unlike her mother, she had an uncanny patience. It was part of what made her such a good speech therapist. She worked for the Del Rio Independ-ent School District and took on adult clients in a small office that she and her husband Dennis had created in their home. She loved her work.

Marilyn had elected to remain in Del Rio, where her parents had settled when her father had retired from the Air Force. Fol-lowing her graduation from Del Rio High School, she completed her education at Angelo State University, and she married Dennis Duncan, whom she had met and fallen in love with while he was still stationed at Laughlin Air Force Base in Del Rio.

Padre was so glad Marilyn had Dennis. Just to think of Dennis now made Padre feel a little better. He would be good for Marilyn now, as he had always been. He would be there for Midge, too. He was rock solid. His years in the Air Force gave him a strong sense of discipline in his life. He loved his new vocation as an environmental engineer. He felt like he was doing something for the common good, even though he often had to deal with ignorance and resistance from a wide variety of people. Dennis was a good husband and a great dad to Mike.

Padre smiled. He remembered the old British golf story about the chip shot. Asked to give an opinion on a particular chip shot, a wag said, "Well, I'd say it's what we call a son in law chip shot; it's okay, but we had hoped for more." Padre thought to himself, "I just couldn't hope for more than Dennis."

Then there was Mike. He was Padre's only grandchild. He was now twelve, soon to be thirteen. He was the apple of Padre's eye. And, in Padre's eyes, Mike could do no wrong, even if Mike's mother did point out a few glaring exceptions to Padre's assessment. Mike was also a baseball player, and a good one.

Chapter Seven

It suddenly dawned on Padre that he might miss Mike's next game. It was tomorrow evening. He cringed. He had never missed one of Mike's games. Never! Then he began to laugh at himself. It just occurred to him that he just felt more disappointment about missing Mike's next game than he had about the possibility of missing the rest of his life. "Baseball fans really are crazy, aren't we?" He said to the barred window on his outside wall.

Padre remembered Mike's last game. He didn't see how tomorrow's game could possibly be any better than that game.

It was the bottom of the ninth. Mike's team was trailing by one run. They already had two outs, and Kevin, their weakest batter, stepped up to the plate. His team mates closed their eyes and wrinkled their noses. When Kevin batted, he looked like he was waving the bat to get someone's attention. The only hit he had gotten all season was when he got the bat in the way of the ball and it turned into an inadvertent bunt toward the pitcher's mound. The pitcher was so surprised that Kevin had hit the ball that he was stunned. He just stood still and blinked for a moment too long. By the time he had recovered and gotten to the ball to throw the runner out at first base, the ecstatic Kevin had already made it well into right field, jumping up and down for the last twenty yards. It was the high point of his life.

There was, however, the matter of two outs. But, at least, they did have a runner, they had Mike, and Mike came up to bat. The pitcher, a twelve year old boy almost six feet tall who could throw the baseball eighty mile an hour, stared at Mike (Intimidation begins early.), and then got a wry grin on his face. He knew that all he had to do was get Mike out and the game was his. How about doing it with just three pitches? At worst, get Mike to hit a ground ball or a pop up. Piece of cake!

Mike had other ideas. He knew the game rested clearly on his shoulders. If he could just get the runner across the plate, they could get into extra innings, and they might have a chance at that point. Just hit the ball somewhere in play. He looked over by third base to get the sign from his coach. The sign read, "Take the first pitch; maybe we can get him behind in the count and rattle him." Mike took the first pitch. It was a fastball right down the heart of his strike zone. The plan didn't work. Now what? The new sign was different. "Hit it, but only if it's a good pitch." Mike wasn't surprised. That was the sermon his coach preached every day. In other words, don't swing at bad pitches, but, if it's good, hit it. Mike dug in. The pitcher was determined to get the second strike and make Mike afraid not to swing at whatever he threw next time. He came again with his best fastball. This time, Mike was ready. He caught it flush with just enough of an upward movement of the bat to launch it over the left field fence.

Mike's team stormed the field. They managed to pick him up, at least for a few seconds. It was a sweet victory. Everyone was very proud of Mike. But no one was prouder than Padre. He too stormed the field, found Mike and gave him a big bear hug.

Chapter Eight

Padre was savoring that special moment when his reverie was broken by the sound of the lock on his door as it was being opened. An electrical charge went through his body. The door opened. Padre was expecting Diego, but the young Hispanic man entering the room carrying what was obviously Padre's supper was not Diego.

Padre looked carefully at the young man. He looked strangely familiar. Padre squinted his eyes. Then it hit him, and he said, "Raul? Raul? Is that you?"

The young man looked sympathetically at Padre, smiled weakly, and said, "Yes Padre. It's me. Raul. You remember me?"

"I do. Of course, I do. I remember you. But you were only fifteen then. How old are you now?"

"I'm twenty-two now."

"Well, you certainly have grown into a fine young man."

"Young man, yes. Fine? I'm not so sure about that."

Padre looked puzzled, but he let the matter drop. "I remember the summer we met. Do you remember that summer?"

"I do. I remember it well. You came to my Colonia with the church group from Jackson Lake, Texas."

"Lake Jackson," Padre gently corrected Raul.

You met with us in the evenings for a whole week, and you talked to us about Jesus. You read the bible to us, and you explained what the bible meant for us. You prayed with us and for us. No one had ever done all that for us. How could I not remember you? I've never forgotten those evening talks with you."

"Do you remember the question I asked your group?"

"I do. You looked us right in the eyes, and you asked us where we wanted to be ten years from now. I remember that well. That question stuck in my mind, and it helped me find enough strength to get out of the Colonia."

"Well, do you remember the answer you gave me that evening?"

"I do. I told you I wanted to be in Dallas."

"Well, did you ever make it to Dallas?"

"I did."

"What happened to you then?"

"Padre, I'm glad to tell you all that, but I need to tell you something else first."

"What's that?"

"I need to tell you that you're in deep trouble. You cannot even imagine how bad."

"Tell me about it. I have already figured out that I'm a prisoner of a drug cartel, right?"

"Right, but not just any drug cartel, you are a prisoner of the "Diablos." And, their, I mean, our leader, is Diablo Guero. You Anglos call him "The White Devil" because he is a white Mexican."

"Did I hear you say 'our leader?'"

"Si, I mean, yes, you did. I am a member of the cartel. I could lie to you and tell you that I just work for the cartel, or that I am a slave of the cartel, but I cannot lie to you, my friend. I am a member of the cartel."

"How...?"

Raul interrupted Padre. "You need to eat your supper. I can't stay with you too long. Angel got called away to take care of a little matter in Acuna, and I'm filling in for him."

"It's a little matter in Acuna? I doubt it. From what I've already heard about Angel, I would suspect that someone is about to die."

"True. One of our dealers stole from us, and then he lied about it. Diablo Guero will not tolerate stealing and lying. This man will not see another sunrise. I don't know how long it will take Angel to kill him. I just know that I need to be sitting outside your door, without your dishes, when he gets back, or he is going to be suspicious. And, we don't want that."

Padre began eating his supper. He looked up at Raul, began to shake his head gently from side to side, pursed his lips, and asked, "Raul, tell me, how did you end up here? What happened to make you become one of the Diablos?"

Chapter Nine

"Well, Padre, you asked me a while ago if I ever made it to Dallas. I told you I did, but I didn't tell you how hard it was. I didn't tell you what it was like in Dallas. I will tell you now, but I am going to have to tell you quickly, because, as I told you, I need to be sitting outside your locked door when Angel gets back. I think we have plenty of time, but I just don't want to put either of us in danger. Okay?"

"Okay. You be the judge. Leave whenever you need to leave."

"Well, you know how the system works. It took years and years for my mother to save up enough money to hire a coyote. It would not have taken so long, but she wanted enough to make sure that she could take me and my sister Lupe and her husband Jorge with her. We paid him up front, and he told us that he would get us across the border safely and give us directions to Dallas. He said it was just a few miles into Texas, and we believed him.

We came over at night. We crossed over between Del Rio and Brackettville. The crossing was easy. We were really more careful than we needed to be. The Border Patrol was no where in the area. You know, and I know, that they can't patrol the entire border all the time. There is just too much territory. So, we crossed. When morning came, the coyote gave us a map he had drawn himself. It showed us where we were, and it gave us directions to Dallas. According to his map, it was only about a hundred miles at the most to Dallas. We thought that sounded like a long way, but we had made our decision, and we were determined to make it. We set out on foot with a bag of tortillas, a jar of beans and a jug of water.

The land was dry and rough. We had no real trail. We just walked through and around the brush as best we could. Before long, the map was of no real use to us. We just knew that, if we kept the Rio Grande to our backs and followed the sun, that we would be going in the right direction. We were still full of hope and confidence. It was thrilling to be on our way at last. We shared our hopes and dreams with each other as we made our way north.

The morning was beautiful. The sunrise is amazing, even in a god-forsaken wilderness. As the day wore on, the sun became less and less our friend. The heat was oppressive. It was early summer, but it already felt like the middle of August. It was not long before we had exhausted our supplies of food and water. But we kept going.

The first night, and the nights thereafter, we rolled out our blankets and slept on the ground. The ground was a hard bed with a layer of sand on the top. What little wind there was made it possible for us to be cool enough to get some rest. Sleep came quickly, but it never lasted very long at one time. The sounds of the night sounded like thunder to us. We heard every little movement in the brush. Our imaginations went wild. What could it be? A wild animal, a hungry wild animal, or a two-legged animal dressed in the starched uniform of the Border Patrol. We knew that they had changed their name to Customs Border Protection. We laughed at that word "Protection." We needed more in the way of protection than any of the hundreds of officers who would be glad to find us and take us back across the border.

The third day out, we found a friendly rancher. An older Anglo woman answered our knock at her front door. She didn't really smile at us. It was more of a combination of disgust and pity. But she gave us some food and water. Since I was the only one who could speak any English at all, I asked her how far it was to Dallas.

She looked surprised at my question. Then she said, "It's a long way from here to Dallas, a very long way," all the while shaking her head slowly from side to side. Then she mumbled something that sounded like, "Oh, my God, you people, you poor people."

I asked her, "Well, can you tell us which way it is to Dallas?"

"I can," she said. "It's that way," pointing North and East.

We left the friendly woman standing on her front porch. She was still shaking her head from side to side.

At the beginning of the second week, many miles and four more ranches later, my mother got very sick. She complained of pains in her chest and down her left arm. She was having trouble breathing, and she looked very pale. We didn't know what to do. We couldn't take her to a doctor, even if we could find one, or a hospital, even if there was one out where we were, and we couldn't have paid for the services. But the real price for the medical care that she desperately needed was that we would all have been deported immediately. All we knew to do was to make as comfortable a bed for her as we could and let her rest. Her breathing was labored, but then, in just a few minutes, it stopped. She died before our helpless eyes.

We stood in a circle and held hands. Tears rolled down our cheeks. We dug a grave for her in the sand. It was a shallow grave because, once we got down below the sand, the ground was as hard as pottery fired in a kiln. No one said anything about what we thought might happen to her body. We just did the best we could to make a cross out of some dried limbs we found nearby, tying them with the sash that she had worn around her waist. Then we moved on.

The loss of her mother, and her pregnancy were just too much for Maria. She made it one more day, then she and Carlos gave up and turned south for home. They begged me to come with them, but I was not ready to give up my dreams. When morning came again, they set out to retrace their steps, hoping to find the same friendly ranchers who had helped us on our way to Dallas.

I would have died, too, except for the next friendly rancher. His wife was the sweetest woman I had ever met. She not only gave me food and water, she invited me into their home and let me sleep in one of their extra beds. A bed never felt so good! Then, to my amazement, the rancher told me that he was short handed on the ranch, and he needed some help.

The ranch work was hard. I learned to build and rebuild barbed wire fence. The ground is always hard, and digging post holes is back breaking work. The wire is like a snake. The more you handle it, the more it is likely to bite you. Often, I was taken out to a site where fence work needed to be done and left for long hours at a time. I hated it.

I also learned to be something of a cowboy. I got to where I could ride a horse pretty well, but I lack a whole lot being a qualified vaquero. I can rope a calf, if he's slow. I know how to brand cattle. I learned to vaccinate cattle, castrate bull calves and do most everything around a ranch that has to be done. The main thing I learned about ranching is that the work is never over. It is an endless list of things that need to be done.

I lasted a year. By then, I had saved up enough money to buy a bus ticket to Dallas. The bus was hot and crowded, but it beat walking thru the brush. When I got to Dallas, I found out that I was just as alone as I had been out in the brush country building fence. I didn't know anyone. And, no one would give me the time of day, once they had asked if I had "papers." I didn't think I would ever find a job. I had gotten to the point that I was eating once a day and sleeping on a variety of park benches. It was not at all what I thought Dallas would be like.

I finally found a steady job in a car wash. I say "steady." It was steady as long as it wasn't raining. Then I got no hours. Those were tough times. I was living from hand to mouth, with no relief in sight. That's when I met Jorge. He was working at the car wash with me. But there was something different about Jorge. He drove a nice car to work. I walked. He wore nice clothes. I wore the same clothes I brought with me from Mexico. He always seemed to have money. I was always broke. He walked with a bounce in his step. I shuffled along with my head down most of the time.

"Jorge," I finally got enough nerve up to ask. "How'd you manage to buy that sharp car?"

"Oh, Raul, my friend, all it takes is money."

"I know that. But where'd you get the money?"

"Oh, my friend, I can't tell you that, or I'd have to kill you," he said, and laughed and laughed. But he didn't answer my question.

A couple of weeks passed. Then, one day, out of the blue, he said to me, "Raul, my friend, how would you like to make some money, some real money?"

His question sounded like the voice of God to me. Money? Some real money? Well, sure, of course, I'd like to make some real money. I'm not any more interested in working in this car wash the rest of my life the rest of my life than I was working on that cattle ranch out in the middle of nowhere. Yes, a thousand times, yes. I would like to make some real money!" I said instantly.

"Then meet me after we get off work. I'll let you in on my little secret for making some real money."

I couldn't wait. The day dragged by. Finally, quitting time came. I met him at his car. We drove away, and we parked in the shade on a street bordering a city park.

"Raul, what I am going to tell you now you must never tell anyone, do you understand? No one, and, if you do, I will have to kill you. I'm not joking this time. Do you understand?"

I could hardly speak. He was so serious! I knew he was not kidding me. I knew he meant every word he said. I finally mustered a "Yes, I understand. I will never tell anyone."

"But you're telling me," Padre said, looking very puzzled.

"It doesn't matter anymore. Jorge is dead. He was one of those who stole and lied to Diablo Guero. Jorge got greedy. He reached the very bad conclusion that Diablo Guero didn't really need all the money Jorge was making for him in selling drugs on the streets of Dallas. He decided that he would be the one to decide what the split of the profit would be. When Diablo Guero confronted him, he lied. It didn't work. It never works. As I recall, he was Angel's first victim in the service of the Diablos.

Before Jorge died, I went to work for Diablo Guero. Only I didn't know who I was working for. I just went to work with Jorge at the time. He told me he had a valuable contact in Mexico. But I never knew his name. After Jorge died, I was contacted by an Anglo man in Dallas. He called me one night at home. He never gave me his name. And, I don't know it to this day. Nor have I ever heard from him again. He was just a contact person who served a one time purpose. But he told me what to do. I was to go to the Baylor Medical Center and meet someone in the lobby of the Baylor Plaza Hotel at 10:00 a.m. on Tuesday, June 16. I would be told what to do next. I went, and I was approached by a beautiful young Hispanic woman who sat down with me in a far corner of the lobby and told me that she was so pleased about my marriage to her cousin Anna, and that she was so proud and happy to welcome me into the family. Padre, I was not and am not married to anyone, including her cousin Anna. She said, 'Let me give you my cell number,' and she handed me a note that had only a phone number on it. When I called that number, I was told where to meet my contact for my first delivery. I was also told that I was on probation. My contact told me that he wished me success, and he certainly hoped I didn't wind up the way poor Jorge had. I received deliveries and made sales for two years. I know how lucky I have been. I never ran into any problems with any of my contacts. Even more importantly, I have managed to stay out of jail the whole time. The odd part is that my luck was understood by the cartel as success. And, they do love success, because it makes lots of money. I guess my probation period was over when I was invited to meet a 'friend' at the Holiday Inn in

Del Rio. I asked how I would know this person, and I was told that I didn't need to worry about it; my friend would find me. He did. I had never seen him before. But I now know him as Diego, the same Diego who brought you here.

Chapter Ten

Padre was fixated on Raul as he listened to his story of heartbreak and descent into a greedy and vicious subculture that simply destroyed everyone and everything in its way. He winced in response to the knot in his stomach, and his eyes began to fill with tears. He had heard how it happened, but how could it have been avoided? Was there not a way to save Raul from falling into this pit? Is there no way of helping countless other beautiful young people from following the same path?

"I'm sorry, Padre," Raul responded to the disappointment and despair he saw growing rapidly in Padre's countenance.

"No, Raul. I'm sorry. I'm sorry that we have let this happen to you. Now, tell me, is there any way you can extricate yourself from this life?"

"No, Padre," Raul said with his own eyes now filled with similar tears. "I cannot leave. To leave is to die."

"Well," Padre said, while blowing his nose and struggling to regain his composure. "I don't want you to die."

"I don't want you to die either, Padre. You will, once we, I mean they, have no more use for you. But I will try to help you. I'm not sure yet what I can do, but I will try."

"I'm not asking you to put yourself at risk, Raul. I certainly don't want both of us to die."

"Padre," Raul said nervously. But Padre couldn't help himself. He reached out and grabbed Raul in a big bear hug. Then he said, "Raul, let's pray together." Raul was obviously torn. He knew he had stayed too long, but he agreed to the prayer.

Padre and Raul bowed their heads, held hands firmly and Padre prayed. "Our Father, we pray for your help now. I pray for Raul and for his safety. Bless him, and lead him out of this time and place in his life to a better future. And, I pray for myself. I also pray for safe keeping a future free from captivity. Lord, we love you and trust you. We pray in Jesus' name. Amen."

Raul pulled loose quickly and said, "Padre, I've got to go now. I've already stayed too long. Angel could be back anytime." With that announcement, Raul turned and opened the door into the hallway.

"Buenos tardes, Raul," Angel said, a big toothy grin only exaggerating the ugliness of his face. He held the door open so Raul could maneuver through with his tray of dirty dishes.

"Gracias," Raul responded, and he smiled back at Angel. He then walked quickly back to the kitchen.

Angel closed and locked Padre's door and waited for a moment for Raul to get out of sight and sound. He then stepped back and looked at a speaker so small no one would ever notice it. It was tucked away in the texture of the dry wall where the wall meets the ceiling just outside of Padre's new quarters. It was capable of monitoring even the slightest noise from the bedroom. He shook his head as any bystander would who had just watched and heard someone doing something so painfully stupid. Then he grinned again, this time even broader and toothier than ever. He then stepped down the hall, so as not to be heard by anyone, and pulled out his cell phone. His first words were "Diablo Guero, Senor…"

Chapter Eleven

"Why doesn't he answer his cell? I'll bet I've told him a hundred times to be ready for my calls when I'm in San Angelo."

Midge's sister Dorothy chimed in. "I guess you've already tried your land line, true?"

"I have, but I don't get anything there but the answering machine. I don't know what's going on with him. He might be with Ramon. He always turns his cell off when he's visiting with Ramon. I wish I could get the kind of respect Ramon gets. But it may be a little late in life to expect that kind of miracle to take place. "Oh, rats! I'll just try again later."

Later that evening, Midge called again. She got the answering machine again, and when she tried Padre's cell phone, there was no answer there either.

"Dorothy, I'm getting a little concerned. Earl is a little absent minded, and, as I told you earlier, he sometimes shuts off the cell, but this is out of the ordinary. I just hope nothing bad has happened to him. I think I'll call Marilyn and see if she has heard from or even knows where he is."

"No, Mom, I haven't heard from Dad. Was he supposed to call me?"

"No, Honey, he wasn't supposed to call you, but I haven't been able to reach him, and I just thought maybe you had heard from him. Well, if you do hear from him, please call me, no matter how late it is, and I'll do the same for you."

"Okay, Mom, but you're making me a little nervous. Don't you think it's possible that he just went out with Skeeter and some of the other guys for a "guy only evening? If that's the case, I think they'll do a good job of taking care of each other. But I will call you if and when I hear from him. Go to bed, Mom, and get some rest. You've got a long day ahead of you tomorrow. Don't forget I love you, and so does Dad. It'll all work out fine. Just try to relax. Okay?"

"Okay," I guess you're right. I'm probably getting all worked up over nothing. Good night, sweetheart."

"Good night, Mom."

Chapter Twelve

Padre had been lying down, trying to slow his mind and rest his body. He had not had much success, despite his best efforts. He decided that he would be better served by working on his breathing. He got better results. He couldn't relax, but the deep breathing was helping reduce the tightness in his chest. He was beginning to feel some better when the door opened. No knock. No voice, no matter; he couldn't have opened the door anyway. It was Diego.

Diego looked at Padre sprawled out on the bed and said, "No time for sleep now, Padre. You come with me."

Padre's mind flashed. He could still remember the first time he heard that command. "You come with me." He hoped this ride wouldn't be as bumpy as the last one.

"Get up!" Diego barked. "Diablo Guero wants to see you. Now! He doesn't like to wait."

Padre rolled over and let his feet hit the floor. He got up and faced Diego. "No blindfold this time?" He asked.

"No blindfold," Diego responded. "Now, come on, let's go! You walk in front of me at all times. Do not try to escape. It would be the most foolish step you ever took. I will shoot you on the spot. Understand?"

"I understand," Padre said meekly and walked over and took his position between Diego and the open door. His chest was beginning to tighten again, and his mouth was getting that same dry taste he had had earlier in the day

Diego's commands were soft but firm. "Look straight ahead. Walk slowly, and do what I tell you."

Padre did as he was told. He didn't want even to appear foolish. Nor did he have any real choice.

Diego marched Padre down a long hall and instructed him to turn right at a cased opening. Padre immediately found himself looking into a very large living room. There was a huge stone fireplace on the wall in front of him, and there were windows on the sides. He assumed they were windows; they were covered with blinds that were closed, and large draperies were drawn almost closed. The room was well lighted with recessed lighting, but they had been dimmed by a rheostat. The dim lighting made for an eerie feeling.

Standing in front of the fireplace was the strangest looking man Padre had ever seen. He was tall, six feet plus, unusually tall for a Hispanic. He was broad shouldered with a bit of a pot belly, doubtless the result of a generous diet of rich food and drink. But what really shocked Padre was the man's hair. It was snow white. It was not the standard gray gradually turning white of the average Anglo male; it was the white hair of an albino. In fact, he had the classic characteristics of an albino. His skin, although brown, had a bit of a milky look. But his eyes were what made him look totally different from other people. His pupils were a deep red while his irises were blue. Padre couldn't take his eyes off him. And his mouth dropped as if he had seen a ghost. He was frozen in his tracks.

"I am Diablo Guero, Padre. It is my pleasure to welcome you to our humble home. I trust that your travel here and your private room have met or exceeded your expectations. We thank you for paying us this visit. We hope your stay with us will be pleasant. The truth is, Padre, that we need you. We need you very much. You see, we have a small delivery we want you to deliver for us across the border. It's really not that demanding a task. In fact, it should not take any longer than an hour or so. If you are receptive to our plan and cooperate with us, your job will be completed before you know it. You can walk away a free man. Now, that's not a bad deal, is it? If, on the other hand, you choose to be uncooperative and give us trouble, you will not walk away at all. Now, Diego, please show our guest to his seat. For the time being, we'll call it the seat of honor."

Diego took Padre by the arm and guided him over to a chair that was facing a large flat screen TV. He nodded to Padre as to say "You sit here." Padre sat down. His imagination was running wild, but he could not imagine why he was sitting in front of a large TV in this living room. He looked around for a split second and he could see that he was not the lone audience. There were several men spotted around the room, none of whom he would want to meet in a dark alley. He looked for Raul, but he was nowhere in the room.

Diablo Guero continued, "Padre, we all like a good movie, don't you?" Padre sat silent and motionless. Diablo Guero continued, "We'll just call this experience Monday Night Baseball. Yes, I like that. Don't you think that's clever?"

All of the men nodded vigorously and said, in chorus, "Si, Si, Diablo Guero. Very clever!"

The film began without the ordinary credits. The setting was a baseball field. But it was not a major league field. It was the setting for a Little League game. The film began with the game in progress. There was a boy at bat.

Padre squinted his eyes, and then he gasped. The boy at bat was Mike, his Mike, his only grandson Mike. Padre got a huge knot in the pit of his stomach. He began to feel nauseated.

Diablo Guero did the narration. "He's really quite good, isn't he Angel?"

"Oh, Si, Senor, he is very good. He might even make a big league player someday."

"But he would have to live long enough to do that, wouldn't he?"

Angel filled the deafening silence. "Si, Senor, he would have to live many more years."

"And, if he died, like, if he died tomorrow because his grandfather did something stupid, he would never have that opportunity, would he?" Diablo Guero asked.

"No" Angel replied. "It would be gone forever."

"Oh, by the way," Diablo Guero continued. "He's pretty small, Angel, do you think you could hit him with your rifle?"

"No problem, Senor. I could hit him right between the eyes"

"Well, Padre, as they say in America, do you get the picture?" Diablo Guero said, flashing a big smile which gave away the fact that he was very proud of his presentation. "Well, Padre, do you get the picture?"

Padre was in shock. He couldn't speak.

"Well, again, do you get the picture? Say I get the picture. Say it, dammit!"

"I get the picture," Padre said in a voice just barely audible enough to be heard.

"Good!" Diablo Guero responded. "Then we have an understanding. You do what we tell you, and the boy can play lots and lots of baseball."

Padre was a mixture of shock and awe, anger and despair. He sat motionless, still absorbing the demonic dialogue of horrible truth.

"Oh, yes, Diablo Guero continued. "I saw you look around the room for Raul. He was not in the room at the time you looked. Diego, would you bring Raul into the room, por favor?"

"Si, Senor."

Diego motioned to Carlos to come with him. He dutifully followed.

Only moments later, Diego and his helper came into the room with a large metal tray. Carefully placed in the center of the tray was Raul's head.

Everyone in the room was deathly silent. Padre could hear his heart beat, and he was not surprised that his heart was racing. He was then overcome with a profound sense of sadness. He put both hands up to his temples and bowed his head toward his knees. He began to sob.

Diablo Guero was not touched by this generous outflow of sympathy and sorrow. He stood silently for a full minute and let Padre have center stage.

"This is what happens to someone who betrays me," said Diablo Guero, flipping up the fingers of his right hand repeatedly to tell Diego to remove his ghastly display. Diego and Carlos left with the tragic tray even quicker than they had entered.

When Diego returned, Diablo Guero said, "Diego, take Padre back to his room. He has been entertained quite enough, and he needs some time to rest. Tomorrow is going to be a very busy day for him."

Padre couldn't get up by himself. His legs were so wobbly that he couldn't stand without holding on to the back of the chair. Diego motioned for Carlos to come and help him. They took Padre by the arms and dragged him back to his room. Once in the room, they positioned Padre so he could fall back on the bed. Then they swung his legs up on the bed.

"Get some rest, Padre," Diego said, never changing expressions. He and Carlos turned and walked out the door, locking it behind them.

It's my fault, Padre told himself. I kept him too long. He told me more than once he needed to go. But, no, I had to keep asking him questions! Why couldn't I just shut up? He would still be alive! Oh, God forgive me, please forgive me! Raul, please forgive me. I am so sorry!

Padre rolled over on his stomach, buried his face in his pillow and sobbed.

Chapter Thirteen

Midge looked up and down the long runway in Terminal A. "Earl," she said in a muffled voice, "Where in the world are you?" Darn, he was here just a minute ago, and now he's vanished. She walked slowly, looking ahead and then back over her shoulder. She did not see Earl anywhere.

She came upon a small gathering of women in a waiting area to her right. She gathered that they were traveling together. A conference maybe or a convention. Then she heard one ask the one across from her, "Do you and your partner play the Lebensohl Convention?" The woman across from her answered, "Yes, we do, but we don't find very many players who are familiar with it?"

"Bridge!" Midge exclaimed. "My kind of gals!" she said, stepping up to them.

"Yes?" The one nearest her said in a less than welcoming tone.

"I'm looking for my husband, and I was wondering if you might have seen him."

The one who had said the yes said, "It all depends. What does he look like?"

Midge was encouraged and replied, "He's my age, tall, about six one. He's very handsome, graying hair over what at one time was a reddish blonde; very distinguished looking with a beautiful smile and a great sense of humor. He's warm and kind and generous and very loving."

"No, I haven't seen him, but I've seen you. Did you scare him away? Maybe he doesn't want to be found." The little group laughed in concert.

A second eagerly answered the question. She smiled too sweetly and said, "If I find him, can I have him?" The group exploded with more laughter.

An exceedingly fat woman joined the fray. "If I find him, I'll trade you my husband even Steven. You know, you get mine, I get yours." The group found this response hilarious. They all but rolled on the floor.

Midge was fuming. She turned to walk away.

"Hey, a new voice entered the dialogue. "Is there a reward, like maybe a weekend in Miami?" Some of the women were crying they were laughing so hard.

Midge walked away. She moved on down the runway.

"Have you seen my husband?" Midge asked a young woman pushing a stroller with a baby nestled down inside.

"No, I haven't seen your husband. Say, can you help me find my gate?"

"What gate?"

"The gate I need to find to get on my flight to New York."

"I didn't even get to tell you what my husband looks like. May I tell you?"

"No, I don't think so. I really need to find my gate."

"I think you're rude. You don't seem to care whether I find my husband or not. He's about six feet tall, with graying hair. It was red at one time. He's wearing a white shirt and…"

"Lady, I don't give a shit what he's wearing. In fact, I don't care whether or not you ever find him. Personally, I think you're a pain in the ass, and I think they ought to get you out of the way so the rest of us can find our gates and get on with our flights."

"Well, I don't think I've ever run into anyone like you before in my life. Where are you from?"

"Hell, it doesn't matter where I'm from. It only matters where I'm going. I'm going to New York, if you ever get through harassing me."

"I'm not harassing you; I'm just trying to find my husband. I think he might be lost. He doesn't have the best sense of direction. I just thought you might be able to help me."

"Well, I can't. And, if I could, I wouldn't, not after the way you've behaved. Didn't your parents teach you any manners?"

"You're the one who doesn't have any manners, young lady. Your parents would be ashamed of you if they had seen and heard what you have done and said here."

"Leave my parents out of this! I'm going to New York, and, for all I care, you can go to hell!"

Midge turned again and walked still farther down the great runway. She came to a man, a very nice looking man about her age, and she felt more comfortable in her search. "Sir, Oh Sir, Pardon me, but I was just wondering if you had seen my husband."

"What is he wearing?"

"He's wearing a white shirt, unbuttoned collar, and a blue blazer with grey trousers."

"Hmn, I might have seen him. Yeah, that might have been him who just came by a few minutes ago. No, of course not, that man was dressed just like your husband, but he was black."

"Well, thank you, anyway," Midge said, smiling sweetly.

She started to move on when the man said, "You know, you are really very attractive. If you don't find your husband, maybe I could fill in for him."

Midge was shocked, again. "I don't think so," she said, trying to be civil.

She moved on again. Next she came across a group of teenagers wearing green shirts with the lettering "Camp Lonesome Pine" blazoned across the front.

"Excuse me," Midge said, maintaining her discreet demeanor. "I wonder. Have you all seen my husband?"

"No lady. But we have seen everything at Disney World. You and your husband really should go sometime, if you ever find him," one particular large and gangly boy said. "Good luck. Oh! I do have one idea you might try."

"What is that?" Midge asked politely.

"Go to lost and found," the boy said, and his whole group broke out in raucous laughter.

Midge stood motionless in front of the smug teenagers. Then she cried out at the top of her lungs, "Will somebody please help me? Oh God, will you please help me? Please, please, please help me!"

Dorothy heard Midge scream. She jumped out of bed and came running toward Midge's bedroom. In the meantime, Midge had been jerked up into a sitting position in the bed. She was looking around the room in a daze. Her face was beet red. She was trembling. She was perspiring freely, and her nightgown was soaking wet. The clock on the dresser read 6:00 a.m. She turned on the light next to her bed, drew a deep breath, blew it out and said, "Praise God that's over!" She crawled out of bed and made her way into the guest bathroom. She looked in the mirror and said, "Good heavens! Midge, you're a mess!"

Dorothy walked into the bedroom. She saw the empty bed and then the light coming from the bathroom. She called out, "Midge, are you okay?"

"I'm okay," Midge hollered through the bathroom door. She came out and Dorothy ran to her and said, "Are you alright, Sis? You just scared twenty years off my life."

"Yeah, I'm okay, no, not really, I'm worried sick. My imagination has been running wild all night. I just had the mother of all nightmares. I can't even stand the thought that even one of the many things I have imagined might have happened to Earl. Dorothy, I don't want to be rude, but I've got to get on the road home just as soon as I can. I've got to know he's okay. I've got to see him. I feel like we've been separated for a year, not a week"

"Oh, I understand, Sis. I can only imagine how you must feel. I have to tell you now that you have bared your soul to me that I'm just as worried as you are. I didn't want to say anything for fear of upsetting you."

"I appreciate that," Midge said, "But you couldn't upset me anymore than I'm already upset. It's the unknown that just drives me crazy."

"I have a plan," Dorothy said. "I know you may not like it, not at first anyway, but I'm going to tell you anyway."

"I'm listening."

"I don't want you to get out on the highway too soon."

"What do you mean, 'too soon'?"

"I want to give you a good breakfast."

"I'm not hungry!"

"I know. I wouldn't be either, but you need to eat to keep up your strength."

"Okay, but then I need to get on the road."

"Well, not quite."

"No? Why?"

"Because you're going to be making a lot of phone calls this morning, and I want you to make them from here, most of them anyway. I don't think you're safe on the highway with as much as you have on your mind, not to mention the additional risk you take on by trying to make all those calls on a cell phone and drive at the same time, and Sis, let's face it. Your foot is not all that big, but it gets a little heavy from time to time. Look. Have a good breakfast. Make all the calls you want on my phone or yours, your choice, and then take off for home. Okay?"

"Sometimes, I really do think you got all the brains," Midge said meekly.

"No, I didn't, and you know better. I'm worried too, but I'm light years away from being in the situation you're in."

"Thank you. You're the best."

"Hello," Marilyn answered.

"Honey, have you heard anything yet?"

"No, Mom. I've been watching our local news almost nonstop to see if Daddy might have been in an accident. I've called the hospital until they finally told me "Don't call us; we'll call you.""

"Okay, I'm going to call Skeeter and Ramon and see if they know anything. I'll call you back as soon as I know anything."

"Okay, and Mom, I'm praying hard."

"So am I, Sweetheart. Bye."

"Bye."

"Hello," a pleasant voice answered.

"Jane, Midge here."

"Midge, I'd know your voice anywhere. Are you okay? You sound a little upset. Is something wrong?"

"Jane, I'm not sure. Is Skeeter there?"

"Yes. He's out in the garage. Let me go get him. This sounds important."

"It is."

"Hi Midge. It's always a pleasure to hear from you? What can I do for you?"

"Skeeter, I'm on my way home from San Angelo where I've been visiting my sister Dorothy. I've been trying to get a hold of Earl, but I can't seem to reach him on his cell or the land line. Do you know where he is? Is he okay? Skeeter, I'm worried about him."

"Midge, as much as I'd like to help you, I don't think I can. All I can tell you is that I played golf with him yesterday morning at the Club. We finished about 12:30 or 1:00 o'clock, somewhere along in there, and that's the last time I've seen him. I haven't heard from him either."

"Was he feeling okay? Was he in good spirits? Did he mention anything about needing to go somewhere in particular?"

"Well, I can tell you he was feeling great. He beat me like a little toy drum, and he was rubbing it in more than a little. In fact, he offered to give me some lessons. Free. Wasn't that nice of him?"

"So you didn't pick up on anything out of the ordinary?"

"No, not at all, I'm sorry, Midge, I wish I could be of more help."

"That's okay, Skeeter. Just please let me know if you hear anything."

"You can count on it."

"First Presbyterian Church," this is Diana, may I help you?"

"Diana, this is Midge Reynolds. May I speak with Ramon?"

"Sure, Midge, I'll get him."

"Well, Midge. How are you this beautiful day?"

"I'm not doing too well, Ramon."

"Oh, I'm sorry. What's the matter?"

"It's Earl. I can't find him, and his cell phone is no longer working."

"Maybe he just dropped it and broke it. It happens to folks all the time."

"No, I mean I've been trying to reach him since yesterday afternoon, and no one knows where he is."

"He hasn't come home since yesterday?"

"No, and, I'm in San Angelo where I've been visiting my sister, and I'm, I'm getting ..... Ramon, I'm getting worried, and Marilyn has been watching the traffic news and calling the hospital, and no one has seen him. Ramon, what should I do?"

"Call the police, Midge. Tell them when you expect to be home, and have an officer meet you there."

"You don't think they'll think I'm just a crazy old woman who's all worked up over nothing?"

"No, they won't. I'm sorry to say this, but you're not worked up over nothing. You're worked up or worried over something. And we need their help in finding out what that something is."

"Okay, if you think it's the thing to do. Ramon. I trust your judgment. I'll do it right now."

"Midge, if there is anything I can do to help, just let me know, and please keep me posted."

"Thanks, Ramon, I needed to hear everything you've said. I'm ready to talk with the police.

"Del Rio Police, Sergeant Kelly speaking. May I help you?"

"I sure hope so, Sergeant Kelly."

"Ma'am, please identify yourself and your need."

"Oh, yes sir, I'm sorry. I am Mrs. Earl Reynolds, and I think my husband is missing."

"Mrs. Reynolds, what is your husband's name?"

"His name is Earl, but most people call him Padre."

"Padre is your husband?" Sergeant Kelly said in the voice of amazement.

"Yes, Sergeant Kelly, he is, and I think he's missing."

"Mrs. Reynolds, our protocol in these situations is for us to send an officer to meet with you and your family. The officer will explore this matter with you thoroughly, and he or she will determine whether there is cause to pursue it further."

"I understand. When can we do that, Sergeant Kelly?"

"I can have an officer to your home in about thirty minutes. Will that work for you and your family?"

"No, sir, I wish it would, but I'm in San Angelo where I've been visiting my sister, and my daughter, Marilyn, she's a speech therapist, and she's at work, and my son in law Dennis is at work, too. We need a little time to get everyone together, and I still need to drive home."

"You really do need some time. How about noon? I can have someone there at noon. Will that work for you?"

"Oh, yes it will. Oh, thank you, Sergeant. Kelly."

"You're welcome, Mrs. Reynolds, and you take care out there on the highway. You've got a lot on your mind."

"I will. I've already made this promise once to my sister."

"Yes, Ma'am, sounds like you have a good sister."

"I do. I really do."

Chapter Fourteen

The door opened. No knock, just opened. It was Diego again. "You come with me. Diablo Guero wants to see you again," Diego said.

Padre had been sitting on the edge of his bed praying and pondering. He didn't say anything to Diego.

Diego told him, predictably, "Walk in front of me, but not too fast."

Padre obeyed, walking through his bedroom door and waiting for further instructions.

"Same place," Diego said.

The two unlikely companions walked Indian style into the large family room. The ample recessed lights were again dimmed to an eerie semi-darkness. Padre saw that the "family" was already gathered in the family room. He looked around at the grim assembly and could not detect any expressions, good or bad, on the faces of what he knew would be his audience. He did notice that the large portable screen on which he had watched "Monday Night Baseball" was gone.

"Here," Diablo Guero barked at Padre. "Sit!"

Padre felt his chest tighten, his stomach knot up and his mouth dry up all in one motion as he took his seat.

"Padre," Diablo Guero began. "You know, we had great plans for you. Great plans! Plans grande! But we have had to reconsider. And, please know, it is not without giving you our utmost consideration. For example, we have been thinking about your age. Padre. I hate to be the one telling you this, but you are getting old, Very Old. We have a lot riding on the little trip we had planned for you, but you are a big risk for us. You see, we're afraid you might just up and die on us from old age before the mission is complete. And that would be a terrible shame. It could disrupt our whole plan.

We've also decided you might just be a little weak for us. When you left the other time you came in here to see us, Diego and Carlos had to drag you back to your room. A man as weak as you might not be able to make a strenuous trip across the mighty Rio Grande. Again, if you couldn't, there we'd be again with our best laid plan collapsing right along with your miserable body. Then there's the issue of your mind. You never say anything, unless I coach you. I am very confused about you, Padre. I can't decide whether you're just hard of hearing, or you are just plain stupid and don't understand even the simplest of commands. I'd ask you which it is, but I doubt that you would say enough for me to be able to make a decision.

So, what I am telling you is that we don't have any need of you anymore. We've taken a vote, and the vote was unanimous. We all agree that you are just not able to help us. So we are not going to ask you to make the terribly difficult and demanding trip for us.

Oh yes, and as far as your grandson is concerned, you need to know that we have already killed him. We felt that we had a certain right to kill him because of all the trouble and expense we are out on you."

Padre dropped his head, grabbed his temples and began to sob. "Oh, Mike, Mike!

"Oh, Angel, I forgot to ask you, "Was he hard to hit?"

"Oh, no, Diablo Guero, it was easy. Just one shot, as always, and, as always, right between the eyes."

Diablo Guero looked at Padre. He was sinking slowly into the floor. The sobbing had not stopped. In fact, it had passed beyond the point of being controllable. Padre's lungs were now heaving as he exploded in grief.

Diablo Guero walked over and put his hand on Padre's right shoulder. "Hey Padre. Don't take it so hard. I was just kidding. We haven't killed your grandson. Padre, come on. It was just a joke." Diablo began laughing. He was joined by a unanimous outburst of laughter from the audience.

Diablo Guero's demeanor changed immediately. His face lost all expression, then he let out a big gasp of air of disgust and said, "Diego, you and Carlos take this piece of shit out and put it in the pit."

Diego and Carlos moved forward quickly on command and got behind Padre. They reached under his arms and lifted him out of his chair. Padre squirmed in a rotating fashion. They just tightened their hold on him all the more. He continued to struggle as best he could, but his efforts were symbolic at best.

Diego and Carlos dragged Padre out of the room on the opposite side from which he had entered. They dragged him through the kitchen and utility room and out the back door on to a rock walk that had been there a very long time. Padre looked up once they were outside. He looked ahead and he saw the pit. It was in the form of an abandoned water well. It had a circular stone wall some four feet off the ground.

When the trio reached the rock wall of the well, Diego held Padre by supporting him by extending his hands and arms under Padre's arms. Carlos picked up both of Padre's legs and, on a count of three, they dumped him over the edge. Padre screamed as he tumbled to the bottom.

He could hear the snap as well as feel the pain of his femur breaking. He dragged himself up against a wall. The pain took his breath away. The total darkness that engulfed him when he landed began to ease some as light from the opening above contributed to a weird foggy atmosphere.

All of a sudden, he heard a whimpering noise from across his new cylindrical environment. It grew louder.

"Grandpa, grandpa, is that you? Grandpa, I'm hurt. I can't move. Help me!"

Padre raised up and started to make his way toward Mike, but the sharp pain grabbed him and rendered him immobile. "I'm coming, Mike. Just hang on! I'm coming," Padre cried out.

Then he heard it. (If you've ever heard it, you never forget it.) It got louder and louder. It was coming from a huge diamond back rattle snake, coiled up in the middle of their floor. The snake's head was moving slowly from side to side as it probed its surroundings with its tongue.

"Grandpa! Grandpa! Please help me!"

Padre jerked up in his bed. His head snapped back. He was trembling all over, and his clothes were wringing wet with perspiration.

He looked around his room. There was no rattler. There was no Mike. There was no pit. He went to his small bathroom, relieved himself, washed his face with cold water and thanked God that it was only a dream, even if it was a very bad dream.

Chapter Fifteen

"Marilyn, Honey, I've called the police."

"The police?"

"Yes, Ramon suggested I do it. He said we need their help."

"I see, I guess. What are they going to do?"

"Well, for the time being, they're just going to send an officer to our house to interview the family."

"When is this going to happen?"

"Today at noon."

"Today? Today at noon?"

"Yes, Sweetheart, and I need for you and Dennis to be there with me to meet with the officer.

"Mom, I've got a full schedule today. I mean…"

"I understand, Sweetheart, but I really think what we're doing takes precedent over everything."

"You really think he's missing, don't you?"

"I do."

"Okay, then Dennis and I will be there. Actually, I can't really speak for Dennis, but I know he will, if he possibly can."

"Oh, thank you, Sweetheart!"

"Mom, are you still in San Angelo?"

"I am, but I'm going to be leaving soon."

"Okay, but drive carefully; you've got a lot on your mind to distract you."

"I know. I'll be careful."

No sooner had Midge put down the phone, than Dorothy came into the room. "Now listen to me, Sis, I have a few things to tell you."

"Oh?"

"Yes. Well, for one, you have plenty of time to get home. Drive carefully. And, two, don't cross any bridges until you come to them. We don't really know much of anything about what is going on. Imagination can be your best friend or your worst enemy. Just put it on hold and take it one step at a time. It's going to require some patience. Unless you've changed a lot in the last few minutes, you are not all that long on patience. Oh, yes, and one more thing. Fill your tank before you leave for Del Rio."

"Wow! That was a good sermon! Have you ever thought about taking up preaching?"

"Thank you, and, no, I don't have any plans to take up preaching. I'm just very worried about my kid sister."

"I know, and I'm sorry I was a smart ass. I just felt a little like I was about to go off to church camp for the first time, and it got the best of me."

"Well, Midge, I don't have a clue as to what's going on, but I can assure you that it's no church camp."

"I know. I know."

"Now, give me one more hug and get out of here!"

Midge held on to Dorothy much longer than she thought she would.

Dorothy picked up Midge's suitcase, put her arm around her shoulders and said, "I love you, Sis, and I'll be praying for you and for Earl, wherever he is."

Midge said, "I know, and thanks," pulling her handkerchief from her purse and wiping the tears from her eyes.

Midge followed orders and stopped long enough to fill her tank. She buckled her seat belt, took a deep breath and said, just above a whisper, "Okay, let's go find out what's going on with Earl."

When she had San Angelo comfortably in her rear view mirror, she pushed down her accelerator just enough to bring it up two miles an hour above the speed limit.

She was making every effort to curb the impulses of her imagination, giving herself one talking to after another, when there was a loud noise and the right rear corner of her car dropped suddenly. She took her foot off the accelerator immediately and tightened her grips on the steering wheel. She managed to steer off the highway onto the shoulder, and she began to apply her foot to the brake pedal in easy steps. She managed to wind everything down to a controlled stop. She got out of her car and went around to the right rear wheel. It was as she had imagined, a blowout. She looked hopelessly in all four directions. She began a mental inventory of her options. Well, she thought, we've got AAA. They're supposed to help in situations like this. But how long would it take to get someone out here in the middle of nowhere? I could wave someone down, I suppose, but who would I get? An eagle scout or a serial killer? I could try to fix it myself, but I've never changed a tire. Goodness, I can't win for losing!

The word losing stuck in Midge's throat. She had done her best to follow Dorothy's good advice. She had been in a life and death struggle with her imagination ever since she pulled out of Dorothy's driveway. But she was losing the battle. Her head began to spin. What was she going to do now? How in the world was she going to get a tire changed in time to make the most important meeting of her life?

It was just too much! The tears paved the way for great sobs. Her chest was heaving. She succumbed by slumping over on the steering wheel.

"Charlie, that car we just passed back there, the one with the flat on the right rear wheel, did you see that woman in the car? She was slumped over the steering wheel. She might be sick, or even dead. We've got to go back."

Charlie looked ahead for a good spot to make a U turn. He needed a little more space than most vehicles. He was towing a bass boat, and he and Darrell were on their way to do some serious fishing on Lake Amistad. He found a good looking piece of shoulder and turned around easily.

Darrell tapped on Midge's window. She raised clear off her seat, with both elbows flying up at the same time. She looked carefully at the face peering in on her. He wasn't a boy scout, no doubt about that, but he didn't look like a serial killer either. In fact, his fishing shirt and floppy fishing hat made him look rather humorous. She rolled down the window.

"Ma'am," Darrell began. "We noticed you when we came by just a while ago. When we saw you slumped over your steering wheel, we got concerned. Are you okay? Is there anything we can do to help you?"

"I'm okay, sort of. I mean, I'm not hurt or sick or anything like that. But, as you can see, I have a flat, actually a blowout, on my right rear wheel, and I'm in a big hurry to get to Del Rio because my husband is missing, and I'm scheduled to meet with a police officer at noon."

Charlie chimed in, "Wow! No wonder you were slumped over the wheel and crying, right?"

"Right, the only things I could think of to do would take a long time, and I don't have a long time."

"Well, Ma'am, I don't know whether we can get you to Del Rio by noon or not. It's not all that long 'til noon. But we can sure get you on the road again."

"Oh, bless you! You can't imagine how much I would appreciate that."

"Yes Ma'am. How about opening your trunk?"

"My trunk?"

"Yes Ma'am, so we can get to your jack and spare tire."

"Oh sure, of course."

Charlie and Darrell made short work of the tire change. Midge stood by smiling the whole time.

When they had finished and had put everything back where it belonged, Darrell said, "Well, that ought to get you rolling again."

Midge teared up again, but this time the tears were tears of joy. "Will you let me pay you? I'd be glad to."

"Oh no Ma'am, we couldn't let you do that. Just pay it forward."

"Pay it forward? What does that mean?"

"It means that when you find someone in need in the future, you step up to the line and help that person, and that's paying it forward, and maybe that person will pay it forward too, and the world gets to be a better place."

"Thank you, Oh, thank you so much!"

"Ma'am, you're as welcome as a good rain in West Texas. Ma'am, we'll be praying for you, and especially that you find your husband safe and sound."

Midge just nodded up and down, speechless. She started to get back in her car, but she stopped, turned around and walked back to Charlie and Darrell and gave each one a big hug, and said, "Well, gentlemen, if you'll excuse me, I'm going to be back on my way to Del Rio."

Charlie and Darrell just looked at each other and smiled.

Chapter Sixteen

Midge looked at her watch. It read 9:50 a.m. She was shocked. She had no idea that her little set back had taken so much of her valuable time. It's probably a little over a hundred miles still to Del Rio. If I push the speed limit a bit, I can still make it on time. She pushed the accelerator down a little more, but a little more soon became a lot more, and, without even realizing it, she was driving 92 miles an hour. She continued glancing at her watch every so often, feeling good that she was making good time now.

She topped a hill and the descent thrust moved the needle to an even 100 miles an hour. "Whoops!" She said, but it was too late. She first heard the siren and then she looked in her rear view mirror and saw the light show going on behind her.

"Darn," she said. "This is the last thing I need now." But she pulled over on the shoulder and waited for the inevitable.

The state trooper said, "Ma'am, may I see your driver's license and proof of insurance?" Midge easily pulled her driver's license out of her purse, but she had to empty the glove box to find the insurance papers.

"Thank you," the trooper said as he recorded the vital information on his I Pad. He returned the license and the insurance papers to Midge and said, "Ma'am, I clocked you in at an even 100 miles an hour. As a matter of fact, I had a hard time catching up with you. Is there some reason you were driving so fast?"

"Yes, officer, my husband is missing, and I'm on my way home in Del Rio to meet with a police officer to talk about what we can do to find him. My family and I have a meeting scheduled with him for noon today."

"Ma'am, excuse me for just a minute. Just stay here. I'll be right back."

"Del Rio Police, Sergeant Kelly speaking, may I help you?"

"Dancer (Sergeant Kelly's nickname was Dancer because his parents named him after the late Gene Kelly, one of the greatest dancers of all time), I've got a woman stopped who tells me she is on the way to meet with one of your officers at noon today in Del Rio. True or false?"

"True, Tommy, Padre's missing, or at least it looks like he might be."

"This woman's husband is Padre, Padre Reynolds?"

"Yes."

"Enough said, thanks Dancer."

"Mrs. Reynolds, I apologize for the delay, and I hope it doesn't offend you, but I had to confirm your story with the Del Rio Police. I am sorry, and I hope you understand, but, if I escorted you to Del Rio and it turned out that you were trying to make a beauty shop appointment, I'd be in deep trouble."

"No offense taken, officer, I quite understand. Did you say something about an escort?"

"Yes Ma'am."

"I want you to follow me about two car lengths back. And, please don't use your cell phone while we're on the road."

"I won't."

Okay, let's go to Del Rio!"

Tommy got in his cruiser, eased out and around Midge's car, moved onto the highway, gave Midge the opportunity to get two car lengths behind him and burned rubber for the first fifty yards. Midge was shocked but recovered quickly enough to follow suit. They were off and running. They both reached 100 miles an hour in only a matter of seconds.

Chapter Seventeen

Padre couldn't stop thinking about Mike. He remembered when he was born. Padre remembered thinking Mike was a little inconsiderate when he made his grand entry into the world at 2:30 a.m. He also remembered that it was well worth it to miss a little sleep. From the time Mike was an infant to the present day, Padre never missed an opportunity to be with him. Above all, he never missed a ball game. It didn't matter whether it was soccer, about which Padre knew very little but still managed to enjoy, or football, of which Padre was a rabid fan or baseball, which he loved almost as much as football. But, most of all, Padre cherished the fishing trips on Lake Amistad that he and Mike enjoyed together.

He recalled one trip in particular. They had been out on the lake all morning. It was well past the first bite and nearly noon. They stopped for lunch in a protected cove, where they were assured calm water and an absence of boat traffic. They had given thanks, as was their practice, and were just getting into lunch, when Mike stopped eating, took a long look at his grandfather and said, "Grandpa, are you a brave man?"

Padre was stunned. At first, he was speechless. Then he mumbled something like "Well, uh, I don't know, Mike. I've really never thought much about that. Why do you ask?"

"Well, because I don't think I'm brave."

"Really now, why is that?"

"Because I'm afraid of Billy Jorgensen. He's always picking on me and trying to get me to fight him. I don't want to fight him because he's a whole lot bigger than I am, and I know how it will all turn out. So I just avoid him when I can, and I run away when I have to. But I don't like to run away because he always laughs at me and yells, 'Come back here, you little coward, so I can whip your ass,' and then he just laughs and laughs. So I don't think I'm brave at all. What do you think, Grandpa?"

"I think you're just as brave as the next fella. But I think you're a whole lot smarter than most of them. I think you can figure out a way to deal with Billy"

"But Grandpa, I've thought about a lot of things, but I never do any of them. I'm too scared. What do you think I should do?"

"Mike, if I were in your shoes, I think I'd spend some time cultivating a new friend."

"Like who?"

"It's not so much who as it is what."

"I don't understand."

"Mike, what I'm suggesting is that you cultivate a new friend who is bigger, stronger and tougher than Billy. Tell your new friend about your problem with Billy. He'll understand. All he really needs to do is let Billy know that if he doesn't leave you alone, he's going to have to fight him. It will help if the two of you are seen together a few times, especially when Billy sees what good friends you are. He'll get the message loud and clear and he'll leave you alone. The risk is just too great for him."

"You really think that'll work?"

"I know it will, and for three reasons."

"What are those?"

"The first is that Billy is a bully. Bullies always pick on people who are younger or smaller or even nicer, because niceness is sometimes thought of as weakness. The last thing a bully wants is to take on someone his size or, worse yet, bigger and stronger. And, that brings us to the second reason. Mike, bullies aren't brave. They're cowards."

"You mean Billy Jorgensen is a coward?"

"I do."

"Wow! But, Grandpa, you said there were three reasons. What's the third?"

"Mike, the third reason I know it'll work is because it worked for me when I was about your age."

"You got bullied?"

"I did, but it stopped when I told my friend Jim about my problem. Jim was the captain of our football team."

"What did Jim do? Did he whip the bully?"

"I didn't have to. He just hung out with me for a while and let it be known what good friends we had become, which was true. So I got relief from the bully and found a new friend."

"That's a great story. I hope mine turns out so well, but Grandpa, that sounds more like being smart than brave."

"Well, you have a good point, Mike, and brave is a little different."

"What does it mean to be brave? Does it mean you're not ever scared anymore?"

"No, there are always going to be times when we're scared. Being scared happens to everybody, but brave people don't let their fear stop them from doing what they need or even want to do."

"Like what?"

"Mike, do you remember when you jumped off the high diving board at the pool for the first time?"

"Oh, yeah, I remember, like it was yesterday."

"Were you afraid?"

"Grandpa, I was so afraid I thought I was going to wet my pants, but then I realized that they were swimming trunks, and they were already wet."

"So, you were afraid, but you went ahead and jumped?"

"Right."

"Mike, you were very brave, or you would not have jumped."

"I see. I understand now. Thanks, Grandpa."

"You're welcome, Mike."

Padre scratched his head and then said, just under his breath, "Grandpa, are you brave?" He had to answer that question for himself. And the answer had to be yes.

He began to muse. Who is the bravest man who ever lived? The answer was a no brainer for him.

Jesus is the bravest man who ever lived. He faced resistance to his ministry almost from the very beginning. But he bravely pressed forward. Why? Because he knew that he was carrying out a plan his heavenly father had for him. Even under the worst of all circumstances, he would not forsake the plan.

Padre continued to let his mind wander. He thought of Abraham. God had a plan for him too. But it was a plan that would take him out of his very comfortable life on a journey into the unknown. It called for enormous courage on his part. Faith in God and bravery made it possible for him to go forward, and God brought his plan to fruition through him.

Then there was Moses. God had a plan for him too. He wanted Moses to go up against the Pharaoh of Egypt and lead his people out into the wilderness. God promised a land that they could call their own, but it was only a promise when Moses exercised some of the most powerful faith and courage the world has ever known.

Padre suddenly remembered that not all the great men and women of faith are limited to the pages of the Bible. He began to recall the countless number of young Americans he had seen and known personally who put their lives on the line every day in some of the most remote and harshest places on the globe for God and country. He had never ceased to be overwhelmed by their humble but never wavering bravery. He was so proud of them and always felt honored to have known them.

Padre chuckled as he pondered at the absurdity of comparing himself to these great giants of the faith. I'm no Abraham or Moses, he thought. But I am a man, and I am caught up in a war. And, Diablo Guero is every bit as evil as any two bit dictator the United States has had to confront. I do have faith. And, I do have some courage. Only time will tell how much. But what I don't have is a plan. I have let the Diablos intimidate me. And, I have let Diablo Guero get in my head. It's time for me to get off the pity pot. It's time for me to stop grinding on what has happened and begin to think about what is going to happen. It's time for me to come up with a plan.

Padre got down on his knees and put his elbows on the side of the bed. He brought his hands together in a tent formation.

He hadn't done this since he was a child saying his prayers before bed time. He prayed: "Lord, I love you and trust you. But, Lord, I need a plan. Please help me. Please give me a plan. And, make me the brave man you want me to be to carry it out. I pray in Jesus' name. Amen."

Chapter Eighteen .

When Tommy reached the city limits of Del Rio, he turned off both his siren and flashing lights. But he continued to lead Midge to her home. When he arrived at the address she had given him by way of her driver's license, he pulled over against the curb and gave her time to catch up. When she approached his car, he rolled down his window and waved to her as he drove on. She waved back, feeling like that was hardly an appropriate expression of appreciation. He had literally saved her day, and she would be forever grateful. She looked at her watch. It read 12:02 p.m.

Marilyn and Dennis had been watching for her at the front window. When they saw her car, the bolted out the front door and ran to her.

Marilyn threw her arms around her mother, then held her by both shoulders and said, "Mom! I've been trying to call you for the last three hours. Why didn't you answer? I have been so worried about you!"

"I'm sorry, Sweetheart, but I was under orders."

"Orders? Whose orders?"

"Well, actually two sets of orders, one from Dorothy and the other from Tommy."

"What kind of orders? And who's Tommy?"

"Don't turn on your cell phone while you're driving. Tommy is the handsome state trooper who escorted me home."

"Mom, we use our cells all the time when we're driving."

"I know, Honey. But I was driving 100 miles an hour."

"You're not serious, are you? You could have been killed!"

"I know. I could have, but I wasn't. I didn't drive that fast until after I had the blowout."

You had a blowout? Where?"

"Oh, I don't know. Not too far out of San Angelo."

"Who fixed your car?"

"Oh Sweetheart, they were just delightful."

"Who are they?"

"Two men, two of the nicest men I ever met, stopped when they saw me beside the road with the flat tire, and they changed out the tire and got me on my way again."

"Is that when you started driving 100 miles an hour?"

"Well, sort of."

"What does 'sort of mean'?"

"I was driving 100 miles an hour when Tommy stopped me. Tommy pulled me over to give me a ticket."

"A ticket, you got a ticket?"

"No, because he asked me why I was driving so fast and I told him."

"And, he believed you?"

"Yes sort of."

"Another sort of."

"He had to call the Del Rio Police on his radio to check out my story. But, when he found out that I was telling him the truth, he apologized for the wait. He said he had to verify my story to make sure I wasn't just trying to make a beauty shop appointment. He said he couldn't escort me to Del Rio, if I was."

"He escorted you to Del Rio?"

"He did, and he's the reason I got here on time."

"You followed him at 100 miles an hour?"

"I did."

"I understand."

A police cruiser pulled up to the curb and stopped. A young officer who looked to be about Dennis' age stepped out and approached the trio on the driveway. He easily picked out Midge and said, "Mrs. Reynolds, I'm Steve Collier."

Midge nodded to acknowledge his presence, then turned quickly around and motioned with her left hand for everyone to follow her, saying, "Please, let's all go in the house now."

Midge led the foursome into her large formal living room. "Please, be seated," she said, as she put her purse down on the dining room table. "Oh, Dennis, would you get my suitcase out of the backseat, please?"

"Sure," Dennis said, and was back in seconds with the suitcase.

"Thanks," Midge said and breathed a great sigh of relief as she sat down in her favorite chair.

Midge smiled sweetly at her honored guest and said to him, "Officer Collier, we are very glad to see you, and we appreciate your coming very much. Let me introduce my daughter Marilyn and her husband Dennis."

"Hi, Marilyn, it's a pleasure to meet you. 'Denthead,' it's great to see you again."

Midge and Marilyn were shocked. "Denthead?"

Dennis jumped in quickly. "What 'Simon Slick from Punkin' Crick' is saying is that he and I go way back together."

"That's true. Denthead, or Dennis, as you know him, and I were in the Air Force together. In fact, we flew several missions together. And had not been for my incredible skills and split second timing, we would never have made it out of some of those scrapes."

"You just got a little whiff of the slick part. What he says is true, except just the opposite was the case. Without my navigational brilliance, we'd be history now."

"Please, enough!" Marilyn said, holding up both hands as if trying to hold back an avalanche bearing down on her.

"Uh, um," Midge contributed. "May we get down to the business at hand?"

"Yes, Ma'am," Steve said, blushing with embarrassment. "I apologize, Mrs. Reynolds, I just got a little carried away."

"A little!" Dennis chirped.

"Dennis, hush!" Midge said, as if she was talking to as small child or a puppy.

"Steve, may I call you Steve?" Midge asked.

"Oh, please do."

"Good, and you may call me Midge. I'm feeling old enough already, without your calling me Mrs. Reynolds."

"Okay, Midge. Good enough. Let's get started."

"Please do."

"Midge, I am going to ask you, Marilyn and Dennis a lot of questions. Some of them may be a little offensive to you. Please understand that I'm not picking on you all. These are just standard questions as a part of our missing person's protocol."

"We understand," Marilyn said. "You're just doing your job."

"Thanks. We'll begin with some basic information I need."

"We'll do our best to help any way we can," Dennis chimed in.

"I know you will. Okay, here we go. I need a picture of Padre and a brief description from you all. Height, weight, hair color, eye color, any distinguishing features, like birth marks, scars, or anything you can think of that might set him apart, like a limp, for example."

"I'll get you a recent picture," Midge said and stood up.

"Don't go just yet," Steve interrupted.

"I also need the make, model year and color of his vehicle and the license plate number.

Midge said," I'll take care of the paperwork. Marilyn, you and Dennis give Steve a description of your dad," and left the room.

"Well, where to start?" Marilyn began. "He's about 6 feet tall. He weighs about…I don't know, what do you think Dad weighs, Dennis?"

"Oh, he probably weighs about 170-175. He keeps his weight down, Steve. He likes to walk in the mall, and he watches his diet. He's actually in pretty good shape for a man his age."

"And, how old is he?"

"He just turned 65 on his last birthday. Marilyn contributed.

"We could do an amber alert on him," Steve offered.

Midge returned just in time to hear Steve's offer. She bristled. "Steve, he may be missing, but he's not senile"

"I'm sorry. I was just thinking in terms of getting the most coverage, but we'll scrap the amber idea."

"Thank you. Here's everything you asked for."

"His eyes?"

"Blue," Marilyn answered.

"Hair?"

"It was a beautiful reddish blonde at one time," Marilyn mused. There's just a trace of blonde left, but it's essentially white now."

"Any distinguishing characteristics?"

"Well, he's almost always smiling," Midge said.

"Or laughing," Marilyn said. "Steve, he has a great sense of humor, and he can see the humorous side to almost everything. One of his favorite sayings is 'We humans are never more ridiculous than when we are taking ourselves too seriously.' Another one is 'You might as well have fun in life. Nobody's going to get out alive anyway.'"

"He sounds like someone I'd really like to get to know," Steve responded.

Midge teared up as she said, "Steve, I hope and pray that you have that opportunity, and soon."

"Midge, I have some questions now that I must ask you all that I hope you won't find offensive, but I have to ask them."

"We understand. Shoot. Oops! I don't suppose it's ever a good idea to tell a policeman to shoot. But you know what I mean."

"I do, and I won't shoot."

"Good."

"Okay. Most of these should go fairly quickly. Is your husband in good physical health? "

"Yes."

"Is he in good mental health?"

"Yes."

"No signs of depression or any erratic behavior?"

"None."

Steve cleared his throat and asked, "How are things going in your marriage?"

"Our marriage couldn't be better."

"Has he shown any unusual interest in other women?"

"Not that I know of, and I would know."

"Has he been to any high school or college reunions lately?"

"No. I've tried to get him to go, but he just says, "Next time.""

Steve moved on. "Does he have a drinking problem?"

"No. He won't even drink a glass of wine. He says it interferes with his sleep."

"Does he gamble?"

"No. He's too frugal to gamble."

"Marilyn laughed and said, "Mom, Dad's not frugal; he's tight!"

Steve pressed on in the interest of time. "Does he own anyone a large sum of money?"

Midge laughed. "We don't owe anybody any money!"

"Finally, I assume you've contacted all of the people who might have seen him or heard from him, and none of them has any idea where he might be. True?"

"True, and they've all been on the lookout for him, too. Steve, it's like he's just vanished off the face of earth. We don't know anything, good, bad or otherwise. What do you think we should do?"

Steve scratched the hair on the back of his neck, then, said, "Let me help you with the protocol at this point."

"Please do."

"Well, to begin with, we have to make a decision. We have to decide between a general concern for his welfare and the possibility that there has been foul play."

"What does 'foul play" mean?"

"Foul play means that we believe that a crime has been committed."

"What kind of crime?" Marilyn asked as she scooted up to the front of her chair.

"It could be any number of things. The most obvious would be kidnapping or murder."

Three jaws dropped simultaneously as Midge, Marilyn and Dennis looked at each other.

Steve was quick to say, "But we really don't know. That's just speculation."

Marilyn was the first to speak. "What do we do? What can you do?"

Steve took a deep breath and said, "Let's cut to the chase. On the basis of everything you have told me, I believe there is a strong possibility that there is foul play at work here. I am going to recommend that we issue a BOLO that will spread throughout the criminal justice system in Texas and across the country in less than an hour."

Dennis asked, "What's a BOLO?"

"A BOLO means be on the lookout. This is where the helpful information you gave me earlier comes into play. We take your information and put it into two data bases. One is the National Criminal Information Center and the other is the Texas Criminal Information Center."

Steve saw all three family members gasp when he reeled off his standard information. He knew why. It was the dominance of the word "Criminal." They cringed as they began to realize that what had begun as a mere possibility had now grown into very strong probability. Marilyn was stoic. Midge began to cry again, and Dennis pressed his lips and looked at the floor. An awkward silence followed.

Steve broke the spell when he stood up, stretched his back briefly, and said "Folks, time is of the essence here. I am going to leave you now and make my report to our Chief of Police. He will make the final call on what we do, but I can assure you that he is going to proceed with the BOLO."

Midge, Marilyn and Dennis rose and all extended their hands toward Steve. But Midge broke rank and gave Steve a big hug and said, "Thank you, Steve. I know we don't really know anything yet, but you have helped us tremendously by listening and promising us action on our concern. I feel better already knowing we are doing something."

"You're welcome," Steve responded quietly and excused himself.

Marilyn and Dennis were voicing their thanks as Steve made his way quickly out the front door.

As Steve drove away, Midge, Marilyn and Dennis joined hands in a circle. Marilyn voiced the prayer: "O, Lord, we love you and trust you to help us. We ask you now to help everyone who is trying and will try to bring Dad back safely to us. We pray in Jesus' name. Amen."

Chapter Nineteen

"Diego, You do understand how important today's shipment is, don't you?" Diablo Guero asked his right hand man. "We've never made a shipment this large or this valuable before. And, you know why, don't you?"

"I do, Diablo Guero, it's because so many of the mules we have used before were weak and collapsed under the pressure the inspectors and the dogs put on them. They wanted to save their loved ones we were holding, but they still broke down when the time came to be strong."

"You do understand well," Diablo Guero commended Diego. "But the situation is altogether different with the old padre. His fast pass will get him and you through without the inspection, but you must make sure that he understands that, if he makes any kind of move at all to expose you and ruin our mission, you will kill him on the spot."

"I understand also that if I had to kill him at the crossing, my chances of making a clean getaway would be slim and none."

"Now you see the big picture. He can get both of you killed, and he might just be crazy enough to try. So, let me help you. When you prep him, make sure he understands that, if he gives you away, you will not only kill him, we will go ahead and kill his grandson. That should put him on notice that he needs to be a very obedient padre."

"I like that. It makes me feel a lot better about our plan."

"I'll bet it does. Now, let's review the plan one more time."

"Good. That always helps. It can keep us from making silly mistakes."

"You will go across with him the reverse of how you brought him over. Tell him to take you out on Highway 90 toward Brackettville. When you are satisfied that you are out on the open highway, you can come out from under the blanket and watch for the turnoff. Make him drive the speed limit, not too slow or over the limit. The last thing we need is a stop by the DPS. Eduardo will be far enough off the highway so you two will not be seen. Remove the shipment from the Denali. Eduardo will have gasoline, matches and all the tools you two will need. If someone stops to see if you need help, tell them you've had a little car trouble, but that you now have solved the problem. When you have unloaded the full shipment and put it in Eduardo's SUV, and when the way is clear, kill the old padre and put him in the Denali. Then set the Denali on fire. This way there will be no DNA or anything else there to lead to us. Eduardo will have the money in several large grocery bags. He will take you to the back parking lot at HEB, where Carlos will be there to meet you. Do you understand?"

"Yes, I do. Diablo Guero, you are brilliant! What a great plan! I promise you that we will execute it to perfection. We will not disappoint you."

"Good, and, just remember; anything short of perfection is not acceptable."

"I understand."

Diego turned to leave, but Diablo Guero caught him by the arm and said, "Go get Maria .I'm ready for her now."

Diego smiled a devilish grin, nodded his assent and said, "Enjoy!"

"I will. I'm sure."

Chapter Twenty

Steve used his siren and lights to get back to the police station as quickly as he could. He was relieved to see that the chief had just returned from a luncheon meeting with the mayor. He was in his office. Steve knocked on the office door. A gruff voice from within said, "Come in."

Steve walked in and handed his lap top to the man they called Chief. Chief took the lap top and began to read. "Mmn, uh," he mumbled as he read the report. He read it thoroughly but quickly. When he was finished, he handed it back to Steve.

"Collier," he said, "This is the most thorough one of these I've ever read. You know, you really went way beyond our little questionnaire, don't you?"

"Yes, sir, I guess I did, but the questions just kept coming to me the longer we talked. Is that bad?"

"No, Son, it's not bad; it's good, damn good! Collier, has it ever occurred to you that you really should be a lawyer?"

"Well, sir, it has crossed my mind a time or two, but I'm really enjoying my police work."

"Good. Then maybe you'll stay around a while. By the way, you did tell Mrs. .Reynolds that we couldn't consider anyone missing for at least 48 hours, didn't you?"

All of the color left Steve's face. He was struck dumb. "No, sir, I guess I forgot about that. I'm sorry, Chief, I guess I just got caught up in the moment."

"God damn, Son, how the hell could you forget that? It's the foundation on which the entire protocol is built. Let me put it to you this way. The last time I made an exception and issued a BOLO in fewer than 48 hours was when we did one on Shorty Romans. We were just dead sure that ole Shorty had been kidnapped. God only knows why anyone would want Shorty, much less go to all the trouble to kidnap him. Our best theory was that he was probably grabbed up by aliens. It had to be done by some folks who didn't have any idea what a worthless bastard he is. Well, it turned out that it wasn't aliens after all. Shorty had just gone fishing out on the lake. He decided for some reason known only to him and God that he would go exploring up in the Devil's River. You know, like he was the reincarnation of Marco Polo. The poor bastard, he got way the hell up in the river and his outboard motor conked out. Poor ole Shorty sat up there with nothing but a paddle, some beef jerky and warm beer until some pilgrim as stupid as he is came up in there, too. That, in a nutshell, is why we don't do one of these too soon."

Chief was getting as red as a beet. Steve was a little worried about him, but he pressed forward.

"Chief, with all due respect to your good judgment, I've got to say that Padre Reynolds is no Shorty Romans. Chief, Padre

Reynolds is a Presbyterian Minister, a former chaplain in the United States Air Force, and a man held in almost superman human regard on both sides of the border. I have checked him out every way I know how, and he grades out A Plus in every category. I think, no, I believe with all my heart that we should issue a BOLO on him ASAP.

"Okay, Collier, and, by the way, you really are going to make one hell of a lawyer, I'll do it your way, on one condition."

"What is that, sir?"

"Find out if he has a boat. I don't think my heart can stand another one of those Devil's River disasters."

"Yes, sir, I'm on it!"

"Hello, Marilyn?"

"Yes, this is Marilyn, Steve, is that you?"

"Yes Ma'am."

"Do you have any news on Dad? Have you found him?"

"Is that the police, Honey? Have they found Earl?"

"No, Marilyn, I wish I did. Marilyn, does your dad have a boat?"

"Yes, he does."

"Do you know where it is?"

"He keeps it in the garage, but I haven't been out there in a long time. Let me check."

"Thanks."

"Steve, the boat is in the garage. Is there anything else I can help you with?"

"No not at this time."

"Steve, you will call us when you know anything about Dad, right?"

"I will. I promise."

"Well, Chief, he does have a boat, but it's in his garage."

Chief's demeanor changed. His face changed from red to white, almost a ghostly white, and he said, "This looks serious, Collier. "Something is very wrong! I'll issue the BOLO immediately."

"Thanks, Chief."

"You're welcome, Counselor."

Chapter Twenty One

Diablo Guero preened like one of his peacocks as he walked back and forth down the long wall of his master bedroom suite. The wall was covered from top to bottom and end to end with a continuous mirror, which paralleled the length of his king size bed. From time to time, he stopped and turned full face to the mirror. The broad smile on his face was more than ample evidence that he liked what he saw. He was a happy man. He would celebrate his birthday this evening with a gathering of his friends, his only friends, his faithful followers in the cartel. They would share the wealth of today's successful shipment, the largest shipment he had ever made. They would rejoice in their newly acquired wealth. They would party! There would be ample food and drink, mariachis to enrich the atmosphere with their music and women. There would be lots of women, women from the streets who would be highly motivated to make sure his friends had the time of their lives. The women who performed well would be returned to the streets of Acuna tomorrow morning. Those who failed to measure up would come to an unfortunate end.

The celebration would be even bigger and better because today was his birthday. What a way to celebrate! He would preside over the festivities for a while, then, he would quietly excuse himself. He would retreat to his bedroom where Maria would be waiting for him. Ah, Maria! What a birthday present! She was perfect. What a gift! Never had he ravished a woman as beautiful as Maria. They would make love well into the night, and he would finally fall asleep a well satisfied man.

The very thought of Maria excited him. But the thought of today's pay day excited him even more. The heroin and cocaine he would deliver to Eduardo would garner him upwards to two million dollars. He would share the money with his friends, but their shares would be but a small fraction of the total take. But they would be happy, and they would thank him profusely and praise him for his generosity. But he would retain the lion's share, and, after all, he was the lion. He stopped one more time and looked at himself in the giant mirror. What a success he was! What a powerful man he had become! He was adored by his friends and feared by all others.

The banker who served as his custodian for his offshore account would be delighted. He would also be diligent in seeing that Diablo Guero's money got laundered in the most lucrative fashion.

Yes, it would be a great day! It would be a day to remember!

He stopped one more time, looked at his likeness in the adoring mirror and said, "Diablo Guero, you are magnificent! What a man!"

Chapter Twenty Two

"Honey, I've got to get back to work. We've got the big dogs from Dallas here today, and I need to be present when John makes his big presentation. Call me on my cell when you hear something, and I'll come home," Dennis said.

"I understand, Darling. Life goes on. Since we don't know anything to tell people anyway, we have to do business as usual. Go on. I'll call you the minute we know something."

"Nobody has to know that behind my smiling face, I'm praying just as hard as I can."

"We know. So are we. But there doesn't seem to be much else that we can do now."

Dennis and Marilyn shared a quick kiss, and he left for the office.

Midge couldn't sit still. She would sit down, then she was up again. She paced back and forth across the living room.

Marilyn watched as long as she could and finally said, "Mom, have you had anything to eat today?"

"I had breakfast at Dorothy's. My goodness! That seems like a year ago! So much has happened in such a short a time!"

Marilyn motioned with her left hand and said, "Come on, Mom. Let's have lunch."

Midge got up one more time. She had actually set her record for the day by staying seated a full two minutes. She followed Marilyn into the kitchen.

The phone rang. Both women charged toward the phone. Marilyn was a little quicker than her mother and answered.

"Hello."

Midge was standing so close to Marilyn's backside that, had Marilyn taken even a step back, they would both have fallen on the floor.

"Is it the police? Is it Steve? Do they know anything? Have they found Earl? Is he alright?" Midge asked in a speed that would challenge the speed of an assault weapon. Her volume was also far beyond any needed for the short distance between the two women.

Marilyn put her hand over the receiver and said, "No, Mom, it's not Steve. It's Donna, and she wants to talk to you."

Marilyn handed the receiver to Midge. Midge accepted it, but she shook her head from side to side, reflecting her disappointment. "Hi Donna."

Donna said, "Are you okay, Midge? You don't sound quite like yourself. Is something wrong?"

Midge swallowed hard, took a deep breath and said, "It's Earl, Donna, we think he's missing."

"Missing? You mean, like in the whole 'Missing Person' thing? Really? Why do you think so?"

"Well, all we really know is that he hasn't answered his cell phone since night before last. No one we've talked to has seen or heard from him. Donna, it's like he's vanished off the face of the earth!"

"Have you called the police?"

"Yes, Ramon suggested that I call the police. They sent out a nice young man by the name of Steve Collier, who, ironically, just happens to be an old Air Force buddy of Dennis.' He took us through a very thorough questionnaire. I didn't think he'd ever get through asking us questions."

"What kind of questions?"

"You name it - everything from his physical and mental health to the state of our marriage. He sounded like a court room lawyer doing a cross examination. But we understand. He was just doing his job."

"Goodness! And, what did he decide on the basis of your answers? I guess that's how it works, isn't it? "

"It is. But it's a little more complicated than that."

"How so?"

"The real purpose of the questions is to try to determine whether there has been any foul play."

"Foul play, like what?"

"It could be most anything. It might be kidnapping or even murder."

"Murder! Oh, God forbid!"

"My sentiments exactly!"

"Well, what was his conclusion?"

"He thinks there is the very real possibility of foul play, Midge said, and began to sob in heaving convulsions.

"Midge, Midge…" Donna said.

Marilyn took the phone from her mother and said, "Donna, I'm afraid you're just going to have to excuse us. You see, you are the first person outside of our family that Mom has told that there is a possibility that Dad might be dead."

"Oh, Marilyn, I understand, and I'm so sorry. Please let us know when you know anything. Jerry and I will be praying for Earl and for all of you."

"Thanks, Donna. By the way, if you don't mind my asking, what were you calling Mom about?"

"Oh, Jerry and I were just going to invite Midge and Earl to come over Friday evening for dinner and a little Bridge."

"That's nice. Mom will appreciate the invitation. But, as things stand now, our social life as a family is on hold."

"I do understand. I'm going to get off the phone now. I'm going to be hoping that you get a call from the police soon and that it's good news."

"Thanks, Donna. Bye."

"Bye."

Midge was leaning over the kitchen sink. Her elbows were on the counter and her hands were pressing against her temples. She couldn't stop crying.

Marilyn looked at her. She had never seen her mother in such despair. Marilyn's stiff upper lip began to quiver, and she began to cry as she had never cried before. She reached out and turned Midge around and reached around her in a firm but gentle bear hug. They stood in the middle of the kitchen and cried until they couldn't cry any more.

Midge gained some semblance of control first. She freed herself from Marilyn's grasp, stepped back and said, ""How selfish of me! I'm behaving as if I was the only one affected by all of this. Honey, I'm so sorry. She put her arms around Marilyn and held on until Marilyn's sobbing subsided.

Marilyn pulled down a section of paper towel, dried her eyes and blew her nose. She looked her mother in the eyes and said, "Okay, Mom, just like the good old days. I'll fry some bacon. You scramble the eggs."

"Sweetheart, I'm not hungry."

"I know, Mom. I'm not either, but we've got to eat to keep our strength up. The truth is that we don't know how long this nightmare is going to last."

"Okay, you're right," Midge said and began to pull things out of drawers with a vengeance. "Actually, it feels a little better to be doing something constructive. Just waiting is killing me."

"Me too."

Midge poured her scrambled eggs into a bowel. On the way to the breakfast room table with the eggs, she suddenly began trembling, and she dropped the eggs, bowl and all. When the glass bowl shattered, she broke into tears again. Standing over the mess she had made, she said, "Honey, I'm a mess! I just don't know how much longer I can take this not knowing anything."

"I know, Mom. Let's face it. Neither of us is just 'All World' when it comes to patience."

Midge broke into a little smile. "I know, the apple didn't fall from the tree, did it?"

Marilyn smiled too. "Not far at all. Mom, I have an idea."

"I never saw you when you didn't."

"How about a diversion?"

"Diversion, like what?"

"Like going to Mike's game this afternoon."

"What about the police? We can't miss a call from them!"

"I'll call and give Steve my cell number. Besides, if we're not at the game, Mike's going to wonder what's wrong."

"Alright, since you put it that way, I'll go, but not a word of this to Mike, unless we have something to celebrate."

"Okay, sure, I'll tell Dennis not to say anything."

"Honey, I'm exhausted. I know you must be too. Why don't we try lying down and resting for a while?"

"I'm game, although I'd be surprised if either of us goes to sleep."

"I agree, but it might give us a little energy for the rest of the day."

"Sure, let's do it."

Midge laid down on her bed, closed her eyes and let her mind drift back over the years. She remembered so many happy times with Earl. But one not so happy time took center stage. It seemed like yesterday.

"Earl! Earl! I'm bleeding. Help!"

Earl opened his eyes, looked across the bed where Midge should have been then realized that the bathroom light was on. He jumped out of bed and rushed into the bathroom. Midge was lying on the floor in a heap of linen bed clothes. There was blood everywhere. She was shaking like a leaf.

"Honey, I'm having chills. I'm so cold!"

Earl wrapped her in a blanket and said, "We're on our way to the hospital. You're going to be fine, Sweetheart."

"Earl, I think I'm losing the baby, our baby. I'm sorry. I don't know what I've done wrong."

"Sweetheart, you haven't done anything wrong," Earl said, and kissed her on the cheek. "And, we don't know about the baby. Let's just get to the hospital and take it one step at a time.

Earl scooped her up immediately and walked as fast as he could to their car. He put her gently in the back seat, helped her get as comfortable as possible and left for the Base Hospital. When they arrived at the Emergency Room, he ran inside and told the first nurse he saw, "I've got my wife out in the car, and I think she's having a miscarriage!"

The nurse yelled at one of the orderlies to get a wheel chair, and she ran out to the car. She opened the door and took Midge by the hand, saying, "It's okay, Honey, you're going to be just fine."

The nurse and the orderly, with Earl's help, got Midge out of the car and into the wheel chair. They rolled her into the ER. The nurse turned to Earl and said, "Sir, you'll need to wait out here until we get her stabilized. There's just not enough room in there for all of us to be in there while we're working with her."

"I understand," Earl said and took a seat in the waiting room.

After what seemed like eternity to Earl, a Dr. Mitchell came out into the waiting room. "Mr. Reynolds? Is Mr. Reynolds here?"

Earl jumped to his feet and shouted out, "Yes, sir, right here!"

"I'm Dr. Mitchell, Mr. Reynolds, and I've just examined your wife."

"Yes, sir, I know. Is she, is she going to be okay?"

"Yes, sir, she's going to be okay. She's lost a lot of blood, and we're giving her replacement blood now. I expect her to respond quickly. That's the easy part."

"Well, sir, what's the hard part?"

"The hard part is the baby. We're going to take her into surgery and see what the problem is. It should take only a few minutes. There's a surgeon waiting for us now. If you'll excuse me, I have some other patients waiting on me."

Earl nodded his assent. He thought. The baby? He hadn't even been thinking about the baby. All of his thoughts were on Midge.

The back door of the waiting room opened. A young woman in green surgical garb walked in and toward Earl.

"Mr. Reynolds?"

"Yes ma'am. Right here."

"Mr. Reynolds, I'm Dr. Elizabeth Garner. I just did a C-Section on your wife, and she's fine. She will need some more replacement blood and a lot of bed rest, but she's going to be as good as new."

"Oh, thank God!" Earl said. "The baby, what about the baby?"

Dr. Garner paused. She took a deep breath and pursed her lips as if that would make sure the right words came out of her mouth. I'm terribly sorry, Mr. Reynolds, but we couldn't save your baby. It was a classical miscarriage, what some physicians call a spontaneous abortion. I wish I could tell you what caused it, but I don't know. There are a lot of possible causes, but I doubt that spelling them out now would make you feel any better."

Earl looked through his tears at Dr. Garner and said, "Thank you. I know you did everything you could."

Dr. Garner wiped her own tears with her sleeve. "Thank you. Not everyone would be as understanding and kind as you are."

"By the way," Earl said, "What we had, or what would we have had?"

"A little boy," Dr. Garner replied, wiped her eyes again and excused herself.

Earl shook his head from side to side. "I can't believe this happened," he said. "Midge has done everything right. In fact, she's done everything her doctor told her to do and more. How can something like this happen? It's just not fair!"

When Midge was taken to recovery, Earl went in to her bedside. She was crying.

"I'm sorry," she said. I thought I had done everything right."

"You did, Sweetheart. It was not your fault. Please believe that. Dr. Garner told me that it was just one of those things that can happen, and nobody knows quite why. You did the very best anyone could do. It's not fair, but sometimes these things just happen. It hurts, but we'll get over it and move on."

He bent over and hugged her neck and said, "I'm sorry too, Sweetheart. But I am so grateful that you are going to be alright. You are the most important person in the world, and I love you more than you can ever imagine.

"I'm so sorry, Sweetheart. I wanted so much to give you a son."

"I know. That's only one of a million reasons I love you so much. But you know what?"

"What?"

"We'll just try again."

"Yes, we will, but not anytime soon, not unless you want to take a shot at having the next one."

"I'm in no hurry!"

Marilyn was resting, or trying to rest in what was now the guest bedroom. She closed her eyes and began to think about her father. Her memory took over and led her back to her eighteenth birthday. The party had just ended when Marilyn walked up to Midge and said, "Mom, there's something I need to show you."

"Sure, Honey, let me see it."

"Well, I can't exactly do that right now."

"Oh why?"

Marilyn whispered softly, "Because it's a lump in my right breast."

Midge's eyes got big. " Really?"

"Really."

"Let's go into my bedroom and lock the door. You can show me there."

Marilyn followed her mother into the bedroom and began to unbutton her blouse. When she had removed her bra, she took Midge's index finger and put it on the spot of her concern.

"Can you feel it, Mom?"

"I can, Sweetheart. I believe we need to have a doctor look at it. I'll make an appointment with Dr. Jackson.

Dr. Jackson examined Marilyn's breast and said, "Marilyn, it could just be a cist, but we'll need to get a biopsy."

"How do you do that?" Marilyn asked.

"Dr. Jackson responded, "It's really a minor surgical procedure. We just need a tissue sample we can forward to the lab."

"When can we do it?" Midge asked.

"Well, first of all, I don't do these. I'm going to refer you to a colleague. Dr. Carrie Donaldson is an outstanding thoracic surgeon. She will do the biopsy and the surgery, if necessary."

"What kind of surgery?" Marilyn asked.

"A mastectomy," Dr. Donaldson responded and added, "But Marilyn, let's just take this one step at a time. We don't even have a biopsy at this time."

"I told her it could just be a cist," Midge agreed.

"That's always a possibility," Dr. Donaldson concurred.

As Midge and Marilyn were walking down the hall toward the elevator, Marilyn asked, "Mom, what's a mastectomy?"

"A mastectomy, Sweetheart, is when the surgeon removes a breast."

Marilyn stopped. The color left her face, and she asked, "You mean I might lose one of my breasts?"

"Well, you could."

Tears welled up in Marilyn's eyes."

"Sweetheart, remember what the doctor said? Let's not assume anything at this point in time."

"Marilyn, the biopsy does indicate that you have a malignant mass in your right breast. We do need to do a mastectomy. I'll schedule it within the next ten days."

Marilyn swallowed hard. She looked at the floor, then her mother and then at Dr. Donaldson.

Midge took Marilyn's left hand in both of her hands and said to Dr. Donaldson. "Dr. Donaldson, this is not what we hoped for, and it's going to take some time to absorb this news."

"Mrs. Reynolds, I fully understand. But please understand that a mastectomy is a very routine surgery."

Marilyn spoke up and said, "Dr. Donaldson, it may be routine for you, but it's not for me."

"I'm sorry, Marilyn. I didn't mean to make light of your situation. I would never do that. Please forgive me."

Marilyn was stunned. She had never had a doctor ask her for forgiveness. She gathered herself and said, "You're forgiven, if that's even necessary. I know you're just doing your job. It's just that…" Marilyn began to cry.

"We'll be okay, Dr. Donaldson. We just need a little time to let this sink in and get ourselves ready."

"I know. It's a very natural reaction. I'd very likely react the same way. You know the difference between minor and major surgery, don't you?"

"No, I'm afraid we don't"

"Minor surgery is surgery you have. Major surgery is surgery I have."

Midge and Marilyn managed a subdued chuckle. Midge added, "It means a lot to us for you to say you would likely react to this news the same way we are reacting. We're all in the same boat, aren't we?"

"Every way on every day," Dr. Donaldson agreed.

"Earl, I'm worried about Marilyn. She's in her room crying as we speak. This mastectomy thing has really gotten to her. Do you think you could have a little talk with her? It might really help."

"I'm probably not much more than a well- meaning fool, but I'll give it a try." Earl tapped on Marilyn's bedroom door.

"Come in," a weak little voice said.

Earl walked in and saw Marilyn on her bed with her head buried in her pillow. She raised up and rolled over. She was expecting her mother. "Honey, your mother and I are a little worried about you. Are you okay?"

"Not really."

"Well, Sweetheart, you're going to come through this surgery just fine."

"It's not the surgery, Dad. It's what it's going to do to me. It's going to turn me into a freak!"

"You're not going to be a freak, Sweetheart. No more than a soldier returning from combat with only one leg is a freak."

"I know, but this is different!"

"How so?"

"Well, for openers, how am I going to look in a swim suit?"

"You're going to look fine. In fact, you're going to look better than any girl in your school."

"No, I'm not! People are going to stare at me, and some will be cruel and make fun of me."

"Sweetheart, the people who make bras and swim suits make special products that will take care of that problem."

"Really?"

They do, and when you wear your new bra and your new swim suit, no one is going to know that you have had a mastectomy."

"Okay, that's great. But what about when some young man gets interested in me to the point that he wants me to marry him. Do I tell him that I have only one breast?"

"Sure, you tell him."

"But what if that turns him off?"

"Sweetheart, if he's turned off by a little something like that, he's not the one for you."

"Just like that?"

"Yep, just like that."

Marilyn had stopped crying. She pulled out a tissue from the box on her night stand and blew her nose. "I feel so much better!"

"So do I," Earl said and followed with, "Why don't you get dressed and come on out. I'll buy you a coke."

Marilyn grinned and began getting out of bed.

"Midge, do the bra people and the swim suit people make special products for women who've had a mastectomy?"

"Sure, they do. Why do you ask?"

"Well, let's put it this way. If they didn't, you and I would have to get in high gear forming a company that does.

Thirty minutes later, Marilyn looked in on Midge. Midge smiled and said, "How was your nap, Honey?"

"About like yours, Mom."

"Well, I did rest a little, at least, I think I did."

"So did I, a little."

"What do we do now?"

"I have an idea."

"I'm not surprised."

"Let's go shopping."

"Shopping? Are you serious??

"I am. You know the saying, don't you? 'When the going gets tough, the tough go shopping.'"

"Yes, I've heard that, but really?"

"Yes, really, it just might keep us sane."

"Where do you want to go?"

"Oh, just grocery shopping. I was planning to go to HEB this afternoon after work anyway. Why don't we go and see if they have any good specials? Come on, get dressed. It'll do us good, and Steve can reach us there as well as here or anywhere else."

"Okay, but I can't believe I'm doing this."

They pulled out of the driveway in Marilyn's car with Midge holding her chin and shaking her head sideways in disbelief.

Chapter Twenty Three

"Dennis, cast right over there," Padre said. "Yeah, that's good, right up next to those lilies. The big fellas like to hang out in places like this. It gives them a good place to hide out from their enemies. They…

"Oh, my gosh!" Dennis squealed as his rod bent double. He was holding on with both hands as tightly as he could.

"Keep your rod tip up," Padre said. "Don't rush him! He's a big bass, and it's going to take some time to wear him down. Just keep a tight line on him. Your drag will do the work for you. When he comes your way, reel as fast as you can. He'll get tired, and you'll be able to bring him up to the side of the boat," Padre added as he got the landing net out of its holder and got in position to land a monster.

Dennis' eyes were nearly as big as his fish by now, and he was trembling all over. He did, however, follow Padre's directions to the letter. About the time Dennis was wondering who was going to wear out first, the fish or him, the tension on his line began to lessen. The old boy was beginning to play out. It wasn't more than a couple of more minutes until Dennis had his big bass under control. He pulled him up and alongside the boat like he was putting him to bed for the night. Padre immediately pounced on him with the landing net. In one fell swoop, the big bass left the water and joined Dennis and Padre in the boat.

"Oh, man"! Dennis shouted." He's a beauty! Look at him, Earl; isn't he beautiful?"

"Actually, Dennis, I can see him from here," Padre said with a chuckle.

"What do you think he'll weigh?" Dennis said, barely able to contain himself.

"Well, let's just find out," Padre said, rummaging through his tackle box for the small scales he carried with him. Padre worked the hook on the scales through the huge fish's jaw, saying, at the same time, "We're going to be real careful with him. We don't want to lose him." The very thought of losing him sent chills up and down Dennis' spine. "Looks like he'll go about 12 lbs.10 ounces."

"Is that a record?" Dennis asked, still trembling a little.

"No, not quite," Padre said. "But he's sure enough a member of the big fish fraternity. Do you want to mount him?"

"Oh, I don't know about that. Isn't that expensive?"

"I don't know. I've never caught one this large. Why don't I take him to a taxidermist friend of mine and find out?"

"Okay, I mean sure, if you don't mind. I'll be glad to pay for it."

Padre just nodded. Padre called Dennis three weeks later. "Dennis, how about swinging by my house this afternoon after work: I've got something I want to show you."

"Okay, sure. What is it?"

"Oh, I can't tell you now. Just come on by, and you'll see for yourself."

Dennis dropped by as invited. He rang the doorbell, and Earl answered. He had a funny little grin on his face. He shook Dennis' hand vigorously and said, "It's in the family room."

Dennis walked into the family room and, when he saw it on the wall above the mantel his jaw dropped almost to the floor. "Wow" was all he could say. His fish was mounted on a dark walnut board with a rugged grain.

Padre said, "There's only one problem with it, Dennis."

Dennis' face dropped. "What's that?"

Padre's grin spread as he said, "It doesn't belong in this house. It belongs in yours," and he reached up and took it down and handed it to Dennis. He then stepped over to the sofa and picked up a lovely painting, walked over to the mantel and said, Step back over there and tell me when I've got it level."

Dennis was in shock, but he managed to ask, "How much did it cost to have it mounted?"

"Nothing," Padre said. "Not a penny."

Dennis couldn't believe it. "Come on, Earl; nobody does this kind of beautiful work for free."

"Jimmy Carson did," Padre countered.

"Why?"

"Because he wanted to, I guess. And, it may have had something to do with the fact that I married both of his daughters and buried both of his parents, and, by the way, I offered to pay him, but he wouldn't hear of it."

"Earl, I can't begin to tell you how much I appreciate this" Dennis said.

"I can't begin to tell you how much I love you. Dennis, you're the son I never had."

Dennis was crying when he heard a voice calling, "Dennis, Dennis, and louder, Dennis! Are you alright?" His supervisor John Taylor was standing by his chair in the large conference room full of people, very important people.

"Dennis, why don't you and I step outside for a while?"

John took Dennis by the arm and walked him down the hall to John's office. Once Dennis was seated, John closed the door and sat down next to Dennis.

"What's going on, Dennis? Tell me. You can trust me to keep your confidence."

Dennis was still crying when he said, "It's Earl, Padre, to you. John. He's missing, and the police think there's been foul play."

"Damn! No wonder you're upset. When did you learn this?"

"Well, I knew there was a problem this morning when Marilyn's mother called. She was in San Angelo visiting Marilyn's Aunt Dorothy. She hadn't been able to reach him on his cell since the day before. She had called everyone she could think of who might either have heard from him or had seen him. She struck out. John, I'm sorry about disrupting the meeting. I know it's an important meeting, and it's important to me, too, but I guess I couldn't help it. I just started thinking back over my life with Earl. I guess, in many ways, my life began when I met Marilyn and her family.

"That's pretty strong, Dennis."

"I know it is, but it's true."

"John, I never really had any parents, real parents. My father left my mother before I was born. My mother was an alcoholic and couldn't take care of herself, much less me. CPS took me away from her when I was just a toddler, and I lived in one foster home after another until I was old enough to enlist in the Air Force. In a nutshell, Earl and Midge Reynolds are the parents I never had."

"I understand, Dennis. I want you to take the rest of the day off, and whatever time after today you need, and go and be with your family. My only request is that you let me know just as soon as you hear anything."

"I will, John, and thank you."

"One more thing Dennis."

"Yes, sir"

"I'll be praying for Padre and all of you just as hard as I can."

"Thank you," Dennis said again, got up, wiped his eyes and left quietly through an exit far removed from the conference room.

Chapter Twenty Four

The door opened. No knock, it just opened. Diego walked in and said, "We need to go over the plan."

Padre, who had been resting on his bed, sat up and looked Diego in the eyes. Diego never changed expression.

"Listen very carefully, Padre. Your life depends on it." Diego began. Padre stood like a statue. He never blinked or changed expression. "I will put you in the back of the Denali, just like I did in Acuna. You will remain still and quiet. If you do anything suddenly, you will find out that I have a very nervous trigger finger. Do you understand?"

"I do."

"Good. When we get into Acuna, I will stop, and we will trade positions as we did before. You will not get behind the wheel until I tell you. You will drive the legal speed limit. No more, no less. You will obey all traffic laws. In short, you will do nothing that calls attention to us as we travel.

When we come to the crossing, you will proceed as you would on any other day. You will smile. You will greet the attendant. You will show your fast pass, if needed. And, you will proceed with caution and deliberation. You will be on the Spur, and you will take the right fork, putting us on Highway 90, on your way out by Laughlin and toward Brackettville. I will stay under wraps until we are out of the city and in open country. I will be right behind you all the time, and my gun will be pointed at the back of your head.

I will give you plenty of notice when we are approaching our turnoff. It will be on a caliche road to our right. Again, you will drive like you had the Chief of Police following you. Again, I ask you. Do you understand everything I have told you? Do you?"

"I do."

"Do you have any questions about any of this?"

"No."

"Very good, I guess all I have left to tell you is that, if you should decide to be a hero or even a martyr, even if we both die, Diablo Guero will have Angel kill your grandson. I know Diablo Guero well, Padre. You can count on it!"

Padre's self-imposed stoicism gave way to a hard swallow and deep breath when Diego mentioned Mike, but this time, he was able to fight back his tears.

"You will get lunch. Then I will come for you. Take a little siesta, Padre, you've got a big afternoon ahead."

Diego stopped for a moment, twisted his mouth, scratched his head and reviewed quickly his mental check list. Once satisfied that he had covered everything, he turned and left as abruptly as he had entered.

Padre took several deep breaths to celebrate Diego's departure. He walked around the room several times, trying to relax.

He stopped several times as he considered the several steps in his plan. Like Diego, he didn't want to overlook any detail. He began to breathe easier with the feeling that his plan was good.

He stopped. He got down on his knees again beside his bed. He prayed as never before: "O Lord, we've been through some tough times together, but nothing quite like this. I'm asking for your guidance and help in implementing our plan. I love you, and I trust you, Lord. I pray in Jesus' name. Amen."

Padre stood up and stretched his legs. He was just getting limbered up when the door opened again. It was Angel. Padre froze in his tracks. The very sight of the man sent tremors through his entire body. But, this time, his fear was unwarranted.

The most beautiful young Hispanic woman he had ever seen walked into his room carrying his lunch tray. She was not only beautiful, she was beautifully dressed. Padre thought it a little strange that someone from the kitchen would be dressed as if she were on the way to a wedding or a fiesta.

She looked back over her shoulder. Angel had left the door open, and she and Padre both knew that he was just outside listening for every word they spoke. After placing the lunch tray on Padre's bed, she stepped back and lifted the front of her very full skirt up to her chin. Padre was shocked, and he turned a very dark shade of red.

She never hesitated. She reached up to the band of her bikini panties and pulled out a scrap of paper. She handed it immediately to Padre. He was stunned even more when he noticed that she was wearing an engagement ring. He took the piece of paper and looked at it. Not knowing that Padre was bilingual, she had made an effort at English. The words scratched on the paper were "I Maria esclava aqui here, help me ...por favor?"

Padre had not seen the word esclava often, but he knew its meaning. Slave, he thought, she is telling me that she is a slave here, and she wants my help.

The young woman looked intently at Padre as he read her note. Her eyes were filling with tears.

Padre put the paper in his pocket, looked up at her and smiled. He said, "Gracious, Senorita," while nodding his assent.

She again lifted her skirt, but this time it was to dry her tears. Padre looked the other way. He looked back and was treated to her beautiful smile, which was a silent witness to a marvelous combination of relief and joy. She offered a perfunctory "De nada," as she turned and walked out.

Angel stepped aside for her and closed and locked the door behind her.

Chapter Twenty Five

Padre was musing again. I just hate it, he thought, when people think I'm stupid. His mind began to wonder why Diego went into such meticulous detail. He concluded that there must be two reasons. The first was the importance of the mission to Diablo Guero. He obviously had a lot riding on this little trip across the Rio Grande. Padre was custom fitted to do the job for him, but Padre must perform flawlessly. The second, he mused, was that Diablo Guero was as compulsive as he was evil. He had probably done the same grinding drill with Diego, both to make sure Diego understood and to intimidate Diego with the importance of a successful delivery.

Padre's mind was chasing another rabbit or two when the door opened again. No knock, just opened. This time it was Diego.

"Time to go, Padre, or, as they say in war, this is it," Diego said. He stepped forward and said abruptly, "Turn around." Padre obeyed. Diego tied Padre's hands behind him. He put the blind fold over Padre's eyes. Taking Padre by his left arm at the elbow, he said, "Now we are ready to travel."

Carlos was waiting for the twosome outside the door. He took hold of Padre's other arm and the two walked Padre through the sprawling house to and out of the front door. When they came to the Denali, they turned Padre around and backed him up to the lowered tail gate of the Denali.

"We're going to help you get your butt up on the tail gate. Then we want you to help us by working your way in. Lie face down, and be very still. We'll cover you with the blanket and your golf clubs."

Padre did as he was told. His jerky movements revealed just how awkward the effort was for him, but he did it and waited. As promised, the blanket came over him and then the golf clubs were piled on top. He could not remember a time when he had been more uncomfortable. He was just beginning to feel really sorry for himself when he heard that noise again. It was the same shrill screaming noise he heard when he arrived yesterday.

"Get the hell out of the way!" Diego screamed. "You damn peacocks are a pain in the ass. I don't understand why Diablo Guero keeps you around!"

Padre could then hear a commotion as the birds scattered. It was quiet again until he could hear Diego getting into the Denali. The engine started. Diego put the Denali in gear and it eased forward down a driveway that crunched as they moved slowly along. A cattle guard broke the spell, and they were soon moving faster down a rough road, which Padre had guessed to be caliche.

Padre told himself that he needed to get his mind off his misery and begin his mental inventory of the turns they would make on their way into Acuna. Think, Earl, he said to himself over and over. You can't stop thinking for even a minute.

The ride into Acuna seemed shorter than the ride over. Padre mused that he had often said to Midge that it always seemed longer when you were going somewhere new than it did when you went back over the same route. He was pondering this piece of wisdom when the Denali turned again and came to a stop.

Padre could hear and feel the door open. Diego was out of the Denali. He opened the tail gate. He crawled in next to Padre and untied his hands and removed the blind fold. "We are going to change clothes as we did when we came over. Then you are going to back out of here just like I came in. No one watching from a distance will be able to tell that there are two of us. Just remember. If you get excited and try to do something heroic, I will shoot you on the spot. Do you understand?"

"I do," Padre said softly.

Diego said, "Now move by me very slowly."

Padre did as told, trying to adjust to the brilliant sunshine that was beating down on the Denali. He stepped out on the street. It felt so good to stretch for a moment. He waited for his next command.

"You are going to get behind the wheel now. Do not do anything sudden. I have a hair trigger, and I will not hesitate to shoot you if I think you are doing something stupid. Do you understand?"

"I do. And, I won't do anything stupid."

Diego had rolled down the rear window on the driver's side. He could easily shoot Padre as he moved toward the driver side door.

"Close the tail gate, and walk naturally forward to the driver side door and get in."

Padre closed the tail gate, stepped back for a moment and walked as naturally as he could to the driver side door and got in the Denali. He waited again.

"Take a couple of deep breaths," Diego said. "I don't want you to pass out on me, and roll up this window," pointing to the rear window on the driver's side.

Padre obliged. The deep breaths felt good. They also eased a slight tightness he was feeling in his chest.

"Start the engine, put the Denali in forward gear and drive to the end of the next block. When you get there, come to a full stop and then turn left. You will be on your way to the crossing. Do not drive too slowly or exceed the speed limit. Do you understand?"

"I do."

"Then let's go."

Padre felt like he was taking his first driving test. The officer who gave him his test made it very clear to him that one big mistake would cost him his license. In this case, he mused, even one little mistake could cost him his life.

He pulled away from the curb, eased cautiously down to the second corner, waited patiently for the traffic to clear and turned toward the crossing. He had rehearsed again and again how he would approach the crossing. The officer on duty would great him with a big smile. It would behoove him to respond in kind. He tried to remember how long it had been since he had smiled. Then he remembered Maria. Yes, that's what he'd do; when he approached the attendant, he would remember Maria and her beautiful smile. He would make every effort to assure the attendant that today was just another day in the life of a minister/missionary.

"Hey, Padre, how goes it today?" Sergeant Kenneth Lane asked.

"Good day all around, Kenny," Padre and smiled as he thought of Maria's smile.

Kenny waved him through with a huge scooping motion by his right arm and hand and yelled, "Have a good day, Padre."

Padre waved his customary thanks and breathed a huge sigh of relief. He had just cleared the first big hurdle in his plan.

He noted the speed limit on Spur 239 and adjusted his speed to fall just under the limit. He did the same when he made the big curve onto U.S. 90. All was very quiet behind his seat until he began to accelerate. Diego pushed the golf clubs to one side, scooted out from under the blanket and took a position on his knees just behind the driver's seat. He had his gun pointed at the back of Padre's head.

Padre began to look ahead. He could not yet see the key to his plan, but he knew the Brackettville highway well enough that it would not be long. Sure enough, about the time he was beginning to get really nervous, it appeared in the distance. It was a huge Mesquite tree off the right of way to Padre's left. The Mexicans long ago had named it "Padre Grande." The Anglo settlers waffled between "Padre Grande" and "Big Daddy." By any name, it was a huge tree with a massive trunk. As Padre focused on "Padre Grande", he began to muse. Earl, timing is everything here. Let the oncoming traffic clear, and make your move.

The moment an eighteen wheeler in the oncoming lane cleared, Padre mashed the accelerator to the floor. The sudden thrust forward of the Denali sent Diego tumbling backward to the end of the Denali. Diego fired his gun, but the bullet pierced the roof of the Denali about half way to the tail gate. Before Diego could recover, Padre turned the steering wheel hard left with all the power he could muster. The sudden change in thrust threw Diego hard against the left side of the Denali. The Denali's right wheels lifted off the pavement. Padre was now driving a two wheel vehicle as fast as he could make it go. When he left the highway from his opposite lane, the Denali regained its balance, landing on all four wheels and went immediately down through a bar ditch and took out an old barbed wire fence, which hardly affected its speed at all. The Denali hit "Padre Grande" head on.

An older couple from Kerrville, who were returning from a vacation at Lake Amistad, saw the collision take place. They immediately called 911.

Chapter Twenty Six

Officers Darrell Jenkins and Steve Collier were in the general area and caught the call for the Del Rio Police. They sped to the scene.

When Darrell and Steve arrived, they could hardly believe their eyes. They looked at each other, shook their heads and Darrell said, "I've never seen anything like this before." They pulled off the road and made their way very carefully to the crash site. They drove through broken chaparral and uprooted Mesquite seedlings, over turned up rocks and loose sand. The wrecked vehicle was beyond recognition. Darrell called the station and advised them that they had arrived at the scene and would begin their inspection immediately.

They stepped out of their cruiser and walked cautiously toward the Denali. There were hubcaps and broken glass everywhere. They worked their way around to the front of the Denali. "Unbelievable!" Darrell exclaimed. The Denali had hit the giant tree dead center on the tree and the Denali. This produced an eerie scene which depicted the Denali in a virtual bear hug of the tree. The hood had been forced up and back against the windshield. The radiator had ruptured, and engine coolant was spewing into the air, making a ghastly hissing sound.

Steve made his way to the driver's side. He looked in at the older Anglo man behind the wheel. Then he stepped back and looked through the rear door opening where a window once was. He saw a much younger Hispanic man. He was piled up behind the passenger seat. He suddenly had a queasy feeling in his stomach. "Oh, my God! This is Padre Reynolds, and the man behind the seat is his kidnapper!"

"He's breathing, Steve," Darrell said as he crouched down as close to Padre as the air bag would let him. "He's not breathing very well, but he is breathing. I'm going to call for the EMT's." Darrell ran to his cruiser.

Steve began trying to get Padre free from the air bag and the seat belt. Padre looked to Steve like someone who had gotten tangled up in his own parachute and landed without its benefit. He cut the seat belt with his pocket knife and punctured the air bag. It was still difficult to get them off Padre's chest. He noticed that Darrell was right. He was breathing, but his breathing was labored, suggesting that Padre may have sustained some rib and even lung damage. He used his handkerchief to stop some of the bleeding from a whole cluster of superficial lacerations caused by the broken glass. He looked over at the cruiser and then the highway and wished that the ambulance was already there. He had to admit to himself that he had done about all he could.

Darrell returned, and he and Steve looked closely at the man in the back. At first, they thought they detected breathing, but they soon realized that he was not breathing at all. His head and neck were in a grotesque configuration that suggested that the impact had broken his neck. They speculated that since he did not have the benefits of a seat belt or an air bag that, if he had been back from the front seats any distance at all, he would have been propelled like a land to air missile into the back of the passenger seat. It was then that Darrell noticed that there was a 38 caliber revolver on the passenger seat resting in a sea of glass.

"Look here, Collier," he said, pointing to the gun. "What do you make of that?"

Steve had been studying the area where the body of Diego was scrambled in with golf clubs and an old blanket. He scratched his head for a moment, then, said, "Darrell, I think I'm beginning to get the picture."

"Really, how so?"

"Well, what we have here is a kidnapping job that didn't work out for the kidnappers, this one in particular," pointing to the crumpled body of Diego. The gun belonged to him, and he was holding Padre as hostage. In fact, he was using Padre as a mule. This Denali is carrying drugs. We just don't know where they are yet."

"I think you're going to make a good detective, Steve."

"Thanks. But this is the only way this wreck makes sense. Padre Reynolds was not going to lose control of his Denali, cross two lanes of traffic, go through a barbed wire fence, knock down enough vegetation to start a commercial nursery and hit the biggest tree in Val Verde County at full speed just because he was a bad driver. He was trying to save his life, and he wanted also to break up the delivery of the drugs. But, mostly, he was willing to risk his life to save it. Darrell, he planned this crash very carefully. It took more courage than we can even imagine to pull it off."

Darrell was shaking his head in amazement when the ambulance arrived. Two paramedics jumped out and ran to the scene. The driver was a young woman who out ran her slightly overweight partner. "What have we got here, guys?" She hollered as she came to Darrell and Steve.

"Two down," Steve responded, and added, "One is still alive," he said and pointed to Padre, but he's unconscious and in bad shape. The other one is probably dead, but we'll let you make that determination."

Quick as a wink, the young paramedic told her partner, "You examine the driver," and I'll take a look at the one in the back."

As her partner was beginning to examine Padre, she yelled out from the back of the Denali, "This one's dead," and added, "You guys might as well call a funeral home to come and get this body. There's nothing we can do for him."

The paramedic working with Padre was meticulously checking Padre's pulse. He was also watching Padre's breathing pattern very carefully. He looked up at the three who were looking over his shoulder and said, "His pulse is weak, and his breathing is labored. He's suffered a concussion or worse, and I can't tell at this point whether he has any broken bones or not. He very likely has some rib damage and maybe even lung damage. We need to get him to Val Verde Regional as fast as we can."

"What can we do to help?" Darrell asked.

"You can help us get him on the stretcher and into the ambulance," the young woman said. He's not all that heavy, but he is extremely fragile. We don't want to do any more damage. He's got all he can say grace over already."

The two paramedics rolled the stretcher out and down from their ambulance, scooted it over to the driver's side opening and pointed to Darrell and Steve to get on each side. Very slowly, they worked Padre loose from the driver's seat and slid him out and down to the stretcher. He never made a sound. They straightened him out very carefully on the stretcher. The young woman then said, "Okay, guys, let's roll him in and get this show on the road."

Her partner stayed in the ambulance with Padre. When he had an IV underway and she was satisfied that Padre was safe to travel, she crawled out and smiled at Darrell and Steve and said, "Thanks, guys, you made this a lot easier."

She jumped into the ambulance. The siren went on. The lights flashed. She, her partner and Padre were on the highway in a matter of seconds and soon reached maximum speed.

Darrell went to the cruiser to make his initial report to Chief, He took a second or two to organize his thoughts and then went on the radio.

"Dancer, this is Darrell. Do your read me?"

Roger that. I do. Go ahead."

"I need to speak to Chief."

"Hello, Jenkins. Tell me what's going on out there."

"Well, it's not what we thought, Chief."

"No? Then what is it?"

"Well, we thought it was a simple one car collision, one that came about because the driver lost control. But it's not. It's a lot more complicated than that."

"What do you mean by more complicated?"

"The driver was Padre Reynolds, and he was being held hostage by a drug dealer who was using him as a mule. Padre deliberately hit "Padre Grande" head on at what must have been close to full speed."

"Damn! Did anyone survive? It's bound to have been one hell of a collision."

"Padre did survive, barely. He's on his way to the hospital as we speak, but he's in bad shape. He's unconscious, with labored breathing. The paramedics said he had a concussion or worse and probably some rib and maybe lung damage. He's all buggered up with cuts made by flying glass."

"How about the drug dealer?"

"He's dead. He was in the back of Padre's Denali. There are no seats in the back, and the drug dealer had no air bag or seat belt. It looked like the impact broke his neck. Anyway, he's dead as a hammer, and the funeral home folks are coming after him."

"Okay, Jenkins, here's what we're going to do. Listen carefully. I will advise all of the law enforcement agencies about the nature of the collision. I'll call in the DEA. And I want the Texas Rangers involved from the git go. I want you and Collier to secure the site. Don't let anyone in, except a Texas Ranger, not even someone who might look like a deputy sheriff to you, no media people, certainly no rubberneckers, no one. Do you understand?"

"Yes Sir."

"This security provision is especially important until the DEA folks arrive. The drug dealers just might decide to make a run at you two and get the drugs out of the Denali. Stay there until the DEA inspectors are finished ."

"Yes Sir."

"And, Jenkins,"

"Yes Sir?"

"You and Collier are doing a good job. I'm proud of you. One other thing."

"What's that, Sir?"

"Let's all pray for Padre. He just might be the bravest man we've ever known."

"Roger that Sir."

Steve had been standing by the open door of the cruiser. He had heard all of Darrell's side of the conversation. But he asked, "What did he say?"

"He wants us to secure the site and stay here until the DEA people complete their inspection. Under no circumstances, are we to let anyone inside the ribbon. He's concerned that the drug dealers might make a run at us before the DEA folks get here."

"Damn! I never even thought of that as a possibility."

Darrell grinned and said, "Maybe that's why he's the chief and you're not."

Steve laughed and said, "You're right. I'm not the chief, not yet anyway."

"Collier, you're hopeless! Oh, yes. He also said we were doing a good job, and he's proud of us. He asked us to join him in praying for Padre, whom he said just might be the bravest man we've ever known."

"I agree, Steve said.

Steve and Darrell ran the yellow ribbon around the crash site. The location changed in one fell swoop from an accident zone to a crime scene. When they were sure their barrier would hold, Darrell got back in the cruiser and began writing up his report. Both were so absorbed in their respective tasks that they failed to see a state trooper making his way through their newly installed barrier. He walked behind the cruiser, and Darrell never even noticed him. He was on his way toward the wreckage and Steve.

Steve was mesmerized by the Denali. He was studying every detail. He picked up the revolver, unloaded it and put it in his belt. He looked around but didn't see any personal items he thought would belong to Padre. Then he went to the back of the Denali and separated Diego's body from the blanket and the golf clubs. When he had Diego's body ready for transport, he turned his attention to the golf clubs and the blanket. Pretty smart, he mused, hide under the blanket until the time is right and use the golf clubs for decoration that suggested business as usual. They're not stupid. They probably had a good plan in place, but Padre's was just a little better.

Steve was sorting out the golf clubs. He was amazed that the clubs came through the collision unharmed. They looked like they were ready for play.

The state trooper had been watching Steve's careful assessment of the clubs. Steve had not noticed him, and he had not said or done anything to give himself away. When he saw Steve take a practice swing with the pitching wedge, he could contain himself no longer. "Hey, Collier, do you need a caddy? I could give you a few lessons too," he said.

Steve turned around quickly, saw his friend Luke Joiner, blushed and said, "I don't know. Do you think you're man enough to carry this big bag?"

Joiner laughed and said, "Collier, I can carry you and that bag at the same time."

"In your dreams,"

Joiner changed expressions. He looked hard at the wreckage and said, "Looks like someone lost control and had a hell of a one car accident."

"Not really," Steve countered.

"No?"

"No, Luke. This was not an accident."

"A suicide?" Luke asked.

"No, neither. This was a very carefully planned and executed collision."

"Steve, you've got to be kidding me! Nobody in his or her right mind would ever do something like this on purpose. Was the driver mentally ill?"

"Not at all; he is as sane as sane can be. In fact, he's brilliant."

"Brilliant? And, he did this? How about sane and retarded?"

"Nope, none of the above."

"I give up. What happened?"

"It's really very simple. The driver was Padre Reynolds, and…"

"Padre Reynolds did this? Is he alive?"

"eYYYes, he's alive, barely. He's on the way to the hospital. His passenger was a drug dealer who was holding him hostage, using him as a mule."

"What about the drug dealer?"

Steve pointed to the dead body in the back of the Denali and said, "You asked a good question. Just where is the drug dealer? I guess the best answer I can give you is that he's been in hell for about thirty minutes now."

"Padre Reynolds? Wow! I have always thought of him as sort of meek and mild. He's always so nice. But, damn! So much for meek and mild! He's a hell of a man!"

"Yes, he is."

"Well, I'd best be about my routine inspection and report. I don't want the captain to think I've been spending all my time trying to teach you to play golf. Oh, and how about sending us a copy of your report? We'll do the same for you."

"Roger that. Help yourself. Let us know if you have any questions."

"Darrell," Steve said after Luke had left. "We're going to have to do a better job than this. Luke should never ever been permitted inside the barrier."

"I know, and I'm just as embarrassed as you are. We'll do better from now on."

"We will."

Chapter Twenty Seven

Sergeant Jerry Bryan retrieved the fax from the ancient fax machine in the stationhouse. He picked it up routinely. When he read it, his eyes bulged out, and he turned quickly and yelled, "Captain Rodriguez, we've got a BOLO on Padre!"

"On Padre? Padre Reynolds, the pastor/missionary?"

"Yes Sir. That Padre."

Captain Rodriguez took the fax from Sergeant Bryan and went out the front door in a flash. He yelled, "Kenny, Kenny, come here!"

Kenny was working with a suspicious car. He turned and looked toward Captain Rodriguez. But he continued his search and question drill.

"Now, God Dammit!"

"Stay right here," Kenny said to his driver, and he ran to Captain Rodriguez.

"Kenny, we just got a BOLO on Padre Reynolds. Has he come through today?"

"Yes Sir, he has. He came through not fifteen minutes ago."

"He did? Well, did you notice anything out of the ordinary?"

"Not really, same old Padre, friendly, always courteous."

"Nothing strange?"

"Well, now that you put it that way, there was something a little different about him."

"What was that?"

"Well, you know Padre. He's always smiling, and kidding everyone. He always has a twinkle in his eye to give you fair warning for what might be coming next."

"Yes, I do know Padre. I've known him for twenty one years, and what you say is true, so what is the problem?"

"Just little things, Captain. For example, he looked really tired. His eyes were bloodshot, not like he'd been drinking, but like he'd not gotten any sleep. And, he had big bags under his eyes. And, his smile, well, he did smile, but it looked almost forced. There was none of that old spontaneity and spunk we are accustomed to from Padre."

"Good observations, Kenny. That's good work."

"But Sir, I let him go through, and I feel terrible about it."

"Don't. You haven't done anything wrong. We can't stop everyone who has bloodshot eyes or bags .We'd have half the adult population of the world stacked up out here. But what you have told me is very important. There's something wrong. Something very wrong! There's not a doubt in my mind. We need to contact the Del Rio Police, the Sheriff's Office, the DPS and the Texas Rangers and let them know he's come through." With that parting volley, Captain Rodriguez went in and had Sergeant Bryan place personal calls to all of the authorities.

The phone was ringing off the wall at the office of the Texas Rangers in Del Rio. The BOLO had hit earlier, and now calls were pouring in from Customs Border Protection, the Val Verde County Sheriff's Office and the Del Rio Police Department and the Department of Public Safety.

Texas Ranger Juan Garza was the recipient of all of these communications. He was reviewing them when his cell phone rang.

"Juan, you've gotten the BOLO and the mass communication, right?"

"Yes, Chief. I have."

"Juan, I want you on this one. There's a kidnapping, a hostage situation and drugs involved. I've called in the DEA, but I want you to be the primary investigator. What do you say?"

"I'm on it! I'm on my way out the door for "Padre Grande.""

"I knew I could count on you."

"Thanks, Chief. I'll do my best."

"I know you will. You always do, and your best is the best."

"Thanks."

Unlike Luke Joiner, who just happened by the scene, Juan knew exactly where he was going. He jumped into his new red GMC 4x4 pickup with the signature brush guard on the front and, with his siren screaming and his lights blazing, took off for "Padre Grande." In a matter of minutes he was pulling up to the scene.

Steve Collier knew Juan only by reputation, but he had no problem guessing who was getting out of the new pickup and walking his way. Juan was a short, swarthy Hispanic man in his early fifties who wore a white Stetson hat, plaid Western shirts, tight fitting Levis with a wide belt with a large silver buckle and dark brown custom made cowboy boots. He carried a 45 automatic in the holster on his hip. He couldn't have been more impressive if he had been twice as tall.

"I'm Texas Ranger Juan Garza," Juan said, as if an introduction was needed. He extended his right hand to Steve. They shook hands. It was hard to tell whose grip was the stronger.

"Steve Collier," Steve responded. "And, this is my partner, Darrell Jenkins."

"Nice to meet you both," Juan said, and turned and walked toward the wreckage. He stopped for a moment or two and shook his head. "Did anyone survive this?" He asked.

"Padre did, but he's in pretty bad shape. He's on his way to the hospital."

Chapter Twenty Eight

"Amazing! I don't see how anyone could have lived through a crash like this. Was there anyone else with him?"

"Just a drug dealer. He was holding Padre as hostage and using him as a mule to make a big delivery."

Juan's eyes got big. "So this was no accident?"

"No. It was a very carefully planned and executed plan by Padre to save his life and stop the shipment from going through."

"What happened to the drug dealer?"

"He died on impact."

"Good! Juan said. "That's one of those sorry bastards I won't have to kill someday."

"No sir, he's very dead. The funeral home people just came a few minutes ago and hauled him off."

"I heard you say this was a drug shipment, right?"

"Yes sir. But we don't know where it is. We're sure it's in the Denali somewhere, but we don't know where."

"It doesn't matter. I'll call the DEA, and they'll find it, no matter where it is, even if they have to take the Denali apart piece by piece."

"Oh, there's one other thing you need to know."

"What's that?"

"When Padre left here for the hospital he was unconscious. The paramedics said he had sustained a concussion or worse and probably had some rib damage or lung damage, since he was having a hard time breathing."

"I see. Gentlemen, it looks to me like you two have this well under control."

"Well, thank you, Sir. We've done everything we know to do. But our orders are to stay here and secure the site. Our chief has told us not to leave until the DEA folks have completed their search.

"Good for him, and good for you!"

"Is there anything we can do for you?"

"No, but thanks for the offer. I'm going to leave this situation in your good hands. I'm headed to the hospital. I want to talk with Padre just as soon as he is able to talk."

The three men shook hands again. Juan stepped away and then turned around. "Thanks for your good police work," he said and ran to his pickup.

Chapter Twenty Nine

"Mom, this is a really good price on green beans, don't you think?"

"Mom, Mom, Mom! Did you hear me?"

"Oh, yes," Midge said, shaking her head. "I'm sorry, Sweetheart, my heart just isn't in shopping today."

"I know. Your heart is in the same place as mine, but we really need to stay as busy as we can."

"I know. You're right."

Marilyn's cell phone rang. She scooped it up out of her purse like she was drawing a gun in a shootout. "Hello."

"Is that Steve? Has he found Earl? Is he okay?" Midge asked again.

Marilyn put her hand over the phone. "It's Dennis."

"Hi honey, are you okay?"

"Not really. I just couldn't get this thing with Earl off my mind. I broke down crying in an important meeting. I was a mess!"

"Well, what happened?"

"John was so kind. He took me down to his office and listened to me. It really helped. Then he told me to take the rest of the day off. He even told me to take as much time as I needed."

"He's a jewel, isn't he?"

"He is. Have you heard anything from Steve?"

"Not yet. Mom and I are at HEB just trying to stay busy. Just sitting and waiting was driving us both crazy."

"I'm at home. Are you coming home when you finish shopping?"

"Why don't we just plan to meet at Mike's game? Mom and I won't have anything cold, so we really don't need to come home until after the game."

"That's fine. I'll just plan to meet you there. It's at five, right?"

"Yes, and Mike told me this morning that he would be the leadoff batter today. He's really excited about it. I think it makes him feel very important."

"He should feel important. He's the most dependable hitter we have."

"You sound like his father."

"I am. Remember?"

"Oh yes, I remember."

"See you at five."

"Okay."

"I'm always glad to hear from Dennis, but..."

Her cell phone rang again.

"Marilyn, Steve Collier here. I have good news. We have found your dad, and he's alive."

Midge was standing so close to Marilyn that she heard what Steve said. "They've found Earl, and he's alive," she said, and jumped straight up and screamed at the top of her lungs, "Thank you, God, Thank you, God, Thank you, God!"

A husband and wife were shopping on the other end of the same aisle. When Midge went air born and squealed, the man turned to his wife and said, "She must have found a hell of a bargain. Let's go see what it is."

Marilyn regrouped from the shock her mother had given her and said to Steve, "Did he tell you what happened to him?"

"No, he didn't, Marilyn. In fact, he's still unconscious."

"Unconscious? Is he okay? Is he alright?"

"Actually, he's on his way to the hospital."

"What happened, Steve?"

"Marilyn, it's a long story. For now all I can do is assure you that he is alive."

"Okay. If that's the best you can do now, we'll just have to wait. But, Steve, we're on our way to the hospital just as fast as we can get there."

"I understand, but please be careful. One Reynolds in the hospital is more than enough for now."

"Bye, Steve, and thank you."

"You're welcome."

"They found Earl?"

"Yes, Mom, and he's on his way to the hospital."

"The hospital? Is he okay? Is he going to be alright?"

"They don't know yet. He's unconscious."

"Unconscious? Oh, mercy!"

"Come on, Mom, we're on our way to the hospital."

"What about the groceries?"

"Leave them. HEB will know what to do with them."

Chapter Thirty

"Diablo Guero, this is Eduardo. Where is Diego? I've had lots of people stop and ask me if I needed help, but I haven't seen Diego yet. Is there a problem?"

"I, I, don't know. I haven't heard from him. He's been gone long enough to get to you. I'll send Angel out to find him. Just stay where you are, and I'll call you just as soon as I know something."

"Okay, I'll wait."

Diablo Guero stepped out of his bedroom and walked into the den where Angel was playing pool with Carlos. "Angel, I just got a call from Eduardo. He hasn't seen Diego yet. I need for you to go down our route toward Brackettville and see if you can find him. It may be that that old broken down Denali has stranded him by the side of the road. Call me when you find him."

"I'm on the way," Angel said dutifully.

Diablo Guero walked back down the hall, went into his bedroom, and looked into the big mirror. He saw a very worried man looking back at him.

Angel looked up and down the side streets in Acuna. No Diego. He looked equally hard down the dirt roads that intersected Highway 90. No Diego. He was baffled and frustrated by the time he saw "Padre Grande" on the horizon. He looked carefully as he approached the huge tree. He couldn't believe what he saw. He drove by slowly and then pulled out his cell phone and called Diablo Guero. "Diablo Guero, Angel."

"Have you found Diego?"

"I have, but you're not going to like what I am about to tell you."

"Well, tell me anyway!" Diego Guero said, screaming.

"It's a mess," Angel began. "The Denali hit "Padre Grande" head on. It is a terrible wreck. I don't see how anyone could have lived through it. The worst part is that there are DEA agents all over the place. They have the Denali turned over on its side, and they're taking it apart piece by piece. They're taking the steel panels off the underside right now."

Diablo Guero's face flushed with anger. His breathing became heavier as he gritted his teeth. Finally, he said, "Angel, I'm going to have to call you back."

"Okay," Angel said and looked puzzled.

Diego Guero turned off his phone. "That old son of a bitch! He'd rather die than let me get my shipment through. Well, he paid a hell of a price to stop me. I'm glad he's dead! Dammit! Two million dollars down the drain!"

He stood like a statue for a moment, then, he grabbed the reading lamp that was sitting on his night stand and threw it across the room. He walked back and forth in front of his huge mirror then turned, stopped and pounded on a sheet rock wall until he had put his fist through it. He turned around put his out stretched hands on his desk. His head fell on his chest as his eyes filled with tears. He stopped for a few moments, took some deep breaths, and pulled out his cell phone.

"Angel, do you have your rifle with you?"

"I do, Diablo Guero. I always do."

"Angel, I want you to go to the ball park where you videoed padre's grandson. The game begins at five this afternoon, and I want you to get there early enough to get set up before anyone can see you. Park so you can get away quickly. I want you to shoot that boy right between the eyes. Do you understand? I want him dead!"

"I do, Diablo Guero," Angel said. "And I will, right between the eyes, as always."

Chapter Thirty One

The ambulance arrived at the delivery dock of the Emergency Room of the Val Verde Regional Medical Center. The driver jumped out and ran around to the back and opened the door. A nurse and two orderlies were ready and waiting for Padre to arrive. The paramedics rolled the stretcher out and down onto the concrete sidewalk. They rolled it carefully inside the ER, and the two orderlies brought a gurney alongside. The nurse winced as the two burly men lifted Padre up and over onto the gurney. Padre neither winced nor flinched. The orderlies rolled Padre down the long hallway and into ER room 5. They repeated the lifting and locating process.

"Go get Dr. Jordan," Nurse Alice said to one of the orderlies. We need to get him some help as soon as we can. But we need a diagnosis first. The orderly left on his mission.

Dr. Jordan was in his late sixties. He had only begun his ER practice recently, having sold his practice in Uvalde. He said to anyone who would listen that he was tired of the high overhead costs and the paper work that plague a small practice. He was glad to be free of real estate, utility bills, employees and the paper work that had become an end in itself. He was doing what he loved most, practicing medicine.

Dr. Jordan answered his summons quickly. He came into Room 5, took a good look at Padre and shook his head. "He must have been in a horrible accident!" As he began to examine Padre closer, he said, as he moved from step to step, "We'll need an MRI of his head. His breathing is quite labored. We'll need an X-ray of his chest. He very likely has some cracked or broken ribs and could even have a punctured lung. He needs oxygen. He looks dehydrated. He'll need lots of fluids. Put in a catheter."

The nurses had been taking notes as the examination proceeded. They were not surprised when Dr. Jordan said, "I'll order the MRI and the X-ray now. You all finish hooking him up to everything we need to monitor his vitals, and get him started on oxygen. I'll be back in a few minutes, and we can assess how he's responding to some help before we take him back for the tests."

Nurse Janice joined forces with Nurse Alice and they made short work of their assignments. While they were watching Padre and waiting for Dr. Jordan to return, Janice said to Alice, "Was it a car wreck?"

Alice responded, "All I know is what one of the paramedics told me, and that is that he hit "Big Daddy" head on.

"Oh, My Lord!" Janice screamed, "That big Mesquite out on Highway 90?"

"One and the same," Alice responded.

"It's a miracle that he's alive at all."

"It is indeed. But, as we all know, 'God works in mysterious ways.'"

Dr. Jordan returned. He walked over to Padre and looked closely at him. He turned and said to the nurses, "Will you join me in a prayer for our friend here?"

The nurses were stunned. No doctor had ever done that before. But they gathered themselves enough for a collective "Sure,"

"O Lord, we pray now for our friend. Please keep him safe, and make him well. In Jesus' name. Amen."

"Take him for the MRI first."

"Yes Sir," the two nurses said in concert.

Chapter Thirty Two

As they walked into the ER waiting room, Marilyn turned to Midge and said, "Mom, you look a little pale. Are you alright?"

"I'm fine, Honey. It's just that I've never been in a car going 70 miles an hour in a school zone before."

"I'm sorry Mom, but we did make it, didn't we?"

"We did. Thanks to you know who," Midge responded, as she pointed to the ceiling with her right index finger.

Marilyn stepped up to the window and said, "We're here to see Earl Reynolds."

The young woman behind the counter said, "Earl Reynolds?"

"Yes, Earl Reynolds, oh, you may know him as Padre."

"Oh, yes, I'm sorry, of course, Padre. He's in Room 5, but let me check and see if it's okay for you to go back now."

She turned quickly, opened the large double doors and vanished. She was back in five minutes.

"They've taken him back for some tests. You may go back as soon as he is returned to his room. Just have a seat, and I'll call you when it's time."

"What kind of tests?" Midge asked.

"I don't know," the young woman responded.

"And, if you did know, you're not authorized to tell us, are you?"

The young woman blushed and stuttered a bit before saying, "No, I'm not."

"It's okay," Marilyn said. "We can wait. We're actually getting pretty good at it, aren't we, Mom?"

"You may be," Midge replied, "But I think I'm getting worse."

They sat down in the chairs facing the reception window.

Chapter Thirty Three

Angel made several trips up and down the street along the backside of the baseball stadium before he decided to park on the opposite side of the street, facing away from the stadium. This location would let him avoid the stadium crowd and simplify his get a way.

He walked down and around the perimeter fence of the playing field. He was getting anxious when he finally saw his best vantage point. He would set himself up outside the fence behind center field. There was a stand of medium size oak trees and considerable under brush. It would allow him to remain hidden. He could use the trunk of one of the trees to steady his rifle when the time came.

He went back to his pickup and got his rifle. He kept it in a gun case that enabled him to break it down and store it. It also made it possible for the gun and case to look like the average attache case carried by any business person.

He tried to make himself comfortable by sitting behind the largest of the trees. Now, all he had to do was wait until it was time to make the perfect shot: "right between the eyes."

Chapter Thirty Four

Midge and Marilyn were getting more and more restless as they waited. The tension was broken, however, when the outside door to the ER opened and a cowboy walked in. At least, he looked like a cowboy.

Texas Ranger Juan Garza looked around the waiting room and saw that the only occupants were two women, an older woman and a younger woman with a strong resemblance to her mother.

Juan removed his hat as he walked up to the two women. "Mrs. Reynolds?" He said with a bit of question in his voice.

"Yes," Midge replied, somewhat startled that this cowboy would know her name. "I'm Mrs. Reynolds."

"Mrs. Padre Reynolds?"

"Yes, yes. I'm Padre's wife."

"Mrs. Reynolds, my name is Juan Garza. I'm a Texas Ranger."

"Nice to meet you, Mr. Garza. This is my daughter, Marilyn."

"My pleasure, Ma'am"

"Mr. Garza…"

"Please, Ma'am, just call me Juan."

"I will, Juan, if you will call us Midge and Marilyn."

"I will, Midge. Do you know why your husband is here?"

"No! Juan, all we know is that he is alive, and he is a patient here, and he is back there somewhere having some kind of tests, and we don't even know what he's being tested for!"

"I am so sorry."

"Do you know why he's here? "

"Yes, Ma'am, I do."

"Well, for God's sake, please tell us!"

Midge, your husband was kidnapped by a drug cartel. They kidnapped him because they wanted to use him as a mule. Do you know what a mule is?"

"I do. A mule is someone who is used to bring illegal drugs across the border."

"Yes, very good, well, Padre was especially appealing to them because of his fast pass. Do you know what a fast pass is?"

"I do."

"Padre drove his Denali across the border with a drug dealer in the back. The Denali had drugs hidden in it somewhere. We don't know exactly where yet, but we will. The DEA is taking the Denali apart as we speak. The drug dealer was forcing Padre to make the delivery. Padre was smart enough to know that when the cartel was through with him, they would kill him."

"Oh, my!"

"Your husband developed a brilliant plan. He remembered "Padre Grande."

"The big Mesquite out on Highway 90!"

"Yes, the one some people also call "Big Daddy."

"Padre maneuvered the Denali so that he would gain speed suddenly, throwing the drug dealer to the back of the Denali. Then he swerved hard to the left, sending the drug dealer hard against the right side of the Denali. He drove across the highway into a bar ditch, through an old barbed wire fence and a lot of underbrush and collided with "Padre Grande" head on."

"Head on? Oh, my Lord, and he survived! It's a miracle!"

"Yes, Ma'am, I'm not a religious man. I guess you could call me a 'used to be Catholic', but I believe this was a miracle. Midge, God saved your husband, just as sure as we're sitting here. As a matter of fact, I'm thinking about going to Mass on Sunday."

Midge and Marilyn giggled respectfully.

"Juan, how badly is he hurt?"

"I can't answer that one. I suspect that only the doctor will know. That will depend on what those tests you mentioned will tell us. As far as I know, he's still unconscious. All I really know for sure is that he took a terrible blow to the face and chest when he hit the tree."

"Juan, thank you for sharing this with us," Marilyn said.

"I wish I could tell you more."

"We understand. Right now, we're all in the same boat."

"Midge, Marilyn, there is something else I want to tell you."

"Please do," Midge said.

"Your husband and father, Padre, as we know him, is one of the most brilliant and courageous men I've ever known. I did two tours in the Marine Corps in Iraq. He is right up there with the best of the best."

Midge and Marilyn began to cry.

Marilyn said, "It's nice to know that we're not the only ones who think he is the best."

"You're not. You can count on that."

The receptionist had heard that last interchange, and she was crying too. She nodded her head up and down rapidly, wiped her eyes with her handkerchief, and said, "Mrs. Reynolds, you and your daughter may go back now. Please, just follow me. Sir, I'm sorry, but it's family only now. If you'll just wait here for a while, I'll let you know when you can go back too."

"I understand," Juan said, "No problem."

Chapter Thirty Five

The receptionist led Midge and Marilyn to Room 5. She pulled back the privacy curtain and motioned that they could come in. Midge started in and stopped, turned around and said, "We're in the wrong room. That's not Earl."

Nurse Alice said, "I'm sorry, Mrs. Reynolds, but this man is your husband."

Midge and Marilyn were stunned. They stood speechless and looked each other, then at Padre. Both were having trouble breathing.

Alice said, "Mrs. Reynolds, do you need to sit down?"

Midge stood mute with her left hand across her chest and her right arm on top of it with her hand over her mouth.

Marilyn had both thumbs under her chin and her fingers on both sides of her nose.

Midge was feeling faint when Dr. Jordan walked up beside her. She unconsciously reached out and grabbed his left arm for support. He turned immediately and held her steady.

The still unconscious Padre was a maze of tubes and wires. He was tied with a wire or a tube to almost everything in the room. He had a transparent tube providing him oxygen through his nose. There was a variety of machines with various and sundry kinds of gauges. It looked like every electric outlet was filled with a plug for something in the room.

"Please sit down, here, Mrs. Reynolds. You too, Miss…"

"I'm Marilyn, Padre's daughter."

Both women sat down by at the side of the bed.

"I'm Dr. Jordan, Jim Jordan, and I'll be taking care of your husband and father for a while."

Marilyn took a couple of deep breaths and asked, "Dr. Jordan, what did the tests show?"

Dr. Jordan responded, "We did an MRI on him. He doesn't have any brain damage, but he has had a severe concussion. We also took X-ray pictures of his chest and lungs. He has two cracked ribs. These are causing the shortness of breath. But we detect no lung damage. And, when he wakes up …"

Midge said, "He will wake up, won't he?"

"Yes," Dr. Jordan gently replied. He will. We have no way of knowing when, but he will wake up. Let me put it this way. He got in a fight with a heavy weight tree, and he got knocked out. But, yes, he will wake up. What I was going to say is that when he wakes up, he's going to be in a lot of pain. We want him to wake up, obviously, but we're going to have to give him large doses of morphine to control the pain. He will go back to sleep, sleep, not unconsciousness. And for at least the next twenty four hours he will sleep a lot. This is the body's way of getting the healing process underway. He was also badly dehydrated, but the IV"s will remedy that deficit. Mrs. Reynolds, your husband has been through a hellish experience, and the wreck was just part of it. He has been under incredible stress, and I doubt that he has slept very much, if any, in the last day or more. But the good news is that he is going to get well. But it's going to take some time."

Midge said, "We have all the time in the world. The main thing is that he's going to get well. Oh, Dr. Jordan, thank you for telling us in words we can understand."

"Mrs. Reynolds, I learned a long time ago that everyone's favorite word in the hospital is 'well.'

"Is there anything we can do?" Marilyn asked. "I mean, other than just sit and wait and pray?"

"Praying is always a good idea," Dr. Jordan said. "As a matter of fact, we three prayed for him before we took him back for tests."

"You did?" Midge said. "Oh, bless you Dr. Jordan. She jumped up and grabbed him in a big hug.

"I believe you're feeling better," Dr. Jordan said with a big smile on his face. "You asked what you can do. You can talk to him."

Dr. Jordan moved closer to Padre. "Like this," he said, and he spoke loudly and clearly into Padre's ear. "Sir, do you hear me?"

There was no response. Midge and Marilyn looked disappointed.

"Sometimes it takes a while," Dr. Jordan said. "Just be patient."

"We'll try," Marilyn said. "Talking and patience."

"I must see another patient now," Dr. Jordan said. "But I'll be checking in on you all from time to time."

Midge and Marilyn sat and looked at each other, as if to say, "Who's going first?" After an awkward pause, Marilyn leaned over the bed and said, "Dad, it's me, Marilyn. Wake up, sleepy head!" There was still no response. Marilyn teared up again and sat down.

Midge stood up, scratched her head, and walked to the bed. She reached down and put her hands firmly on Padre's shoulders and said in a voice heard all the way down the hall, "Okay, Chief, you can't sleep your life away. It's time to get up!" There was no response. She sat down and began to cry again.

"Unh, unh, headache, hurts." Padre opened his eyes. They looked like big pools of blood, but they were open.

Midge and Marilyn jumped straight up. Both women squealed at the top of their lungs, even as the nurses were trying to shush them with a finger over their lips. They grabbed each other and danced in a circle, whooping for joy all the time. Marilyn stopped and kissed Alice on the cheek. Midge did the same to Janice.

Midge and Marilyn were all over Padre, but very gently. They kissed him on his forehead over and over. Then they would give him a break and hug each other.

The groans gradually turned into words, but only a very few at a time. Midge and Marilyn had to get down in his face in order to hear. But they could hear.

"M, M, M, Mike," Padre said.

Midge said, "Mike? He's saying Mike?"

"I think so, Mom."

"M, Mike. Get Mike off field," Padre said.

"Get Mike off the field?" Marilyn said. "Why, Dad?"

"Bad men kill Mike on field. Get him off," Padre said, using up every ounce of energy he had.

"Oh, My God! Bad men are going to kill Mike if we don't get him off the field," Marilyn said.

Padre was spent, but he managed to nod his head up and down.

Marilyn grabbed her purse, kissed her father and mother on the cheek, and left the room in a dead run. She ran as hard as she could until she came to a door marked EXIT. It was not the door she and Midge had used. It led directly to the outside. She could see the parking lot beyond the corner of the building. She ran full speed again to her car, jumped in, started the engine, backed out, turned toward the street and burned rubber to the first stop sign.

Chapter Thirty Six

Marilyn was hardly out the door when Midge tugged at Alice's sleeve. "Alice, there's a Texas Ranger sitting in the waiting room. Please go get him and bring him back in here."

Alice wasn't as fast as Marilyn, but she wasted no time. In a matter of a minute or so, she returned to Room 5, hand and hand with Juan.

"Juan," Marilyn said, "Earl just told us that some bad men are going to try to kill our grandson Mike at the baseball game today."

"Where is the game being played?"

"It's at Roosevelt."

"When does the game begin?"

"Five o'clock."

Juan looked at his watch, then heard a noise from the bed.

"Juan," Padre said as loud as he could, which was barely audible.

Juan rushed to his bedside. "Yes, Padre."

"Angel," Padre said.

Juan's eyes flashed. "I know Angel, Padre, Angel Martinez, He killed my brother Hector. Don't worry about Angel, Padre. I'll take care of him."

Juan turned quickly and left the room as fast as his short legs would carry him.

Padre smiled sweetly through his pain and prayed," Lord," he prayed," I thank you that I am not Angel," and he groaned loud enough to lift Midge up off her chair.

Alice decided it was time for some morphine. She gave Padre a generous dose, and in just a short time he drifted off to sleep.

The very mention of Angel's name raised Juan's blood pressure. An anger that had been marginally repressed for years began to bubble to the surface. He remembered in detail what Angel did to his younger brother. Miguel told him.

"We had just finished our baseball game. We were all in the dugout. It was hot, and we were thirsty. There was one bottle of beer left in the ice chest. We all knew it belonged to Hector, because everyone else had already had at least one. Hector would never take a drink until the game was over. The rest of us would begin as soon as we knew we weren't going back out on the field.

Angel lifted Hector's beer out of the ice chest. He popped the cap off and took a big swig. Hector saw him and said, 'Hey, Angel, that's my beer. You've already had two.'

Angel smirked and said, 'Shut up, Shorty. I'll drink your beer if I want to.'

Hector walked up to Angel and tried to take the bottle away from him. Angel switched the bottle to his left hand and hit Hector right on the nose with his right fist. Hector fell down, but he got right back up. He went into his Golden Gloves mode and knocked Angel down flat on his back. He picked up the partial bottle of beer, took a big swig himself and turned away. Angel was red with rage. He got up, went over to the bat rack, pulled out a bat and hit Hector from behind on his right temple. Hector screamed and went down face first. He never made another sound. Some of us ran to him and realized that he was not breathing. We tried to find a pulse, but he didn't have one. I turned to Angel and said, 'You killed him!'

Angel said, 'You saw it. It was self-defense. And if you tell anyone it was anything else, you'll end up just like Shorty.'

Well, we were all too afraid of Angel to tell the authorities what really happened. So Angel got away with his first murder. There have been a lot more since. Juan, I'm so sorry. Please forgive me.'"

Juan had forgiven Miguel a long time ago. But he had not forgiven Angel, and part of what fueled his drive to become a Texas Ranger was the lingering hope that one day he would have an opportunity to kill Angel.

Chapter Thirty Seven

Marilyn was driving as fast as she could and still maintain control of her car. She had never even looked at her speedometer. She heard a strange sound. She looked in her rear view mirror. A Del Rio Police cruiser was bearing down on her with siren blaring and lights glowing.

"Ah, Hell," she said, "Not now!" She stepped on her brake pedal and looked for a good place to pull over. The officer stepped out of his cruiser, I Pad in hand. He stopped long enough to record her license plate. Then he appeared at her open window.

"Ma'am, I clocked you at 73 miles an hour. Do you realize you're in a school zone? May I see your license and proof of insurance?"

Marilyn slumped over the steering wheel and began to sob. The officer was shocked. "Ma'am, are you alright?"

"No, I'm not alright," Marilyn bristled." My son's life's in danger, and if I don't get to Roosevelt Little League Park as soon as possible, he's going to be shot by an assassin who is a member of a drug cartel. Hell no, I'm not alright!"

The officer looked again at her license, then asked. "Who are you?"

"I'm Padre Reynolds daughter."

The officer's eyes got big and he handed Marilyn her license and insurance certificate. She took them and looked puzzled.

"Follow me, the officer said. "Give me about one car length."

Before Marilyn could say anything, he was gone. The next thing she knew she was following him at 95 miles an hour.

Roosevelt Little League Park was packed. Today's game was a playoff game. Mike's team was undefeated in league play, and today's game was with their toughest rival. The parking lot was packed.

The police officer never turned into the packed parking lot. He stopped at the opening, jumped out of his car and yelled at Marilyn as she pulled up behind him. "Throw me your keys. I'll take care of your car."

Marilyn got out and threw the keys to him even as she broke into a dead run.

Jerry McDermott was videoing the game, as was his practice. His son Trey was the short stop for Mike's team, and he had recorded every game of the season. He would then post them on the internet so every family would have a copy. He was panning the field as Marilyn charged toward the playing field.

The umpire yelled, "Batter Up!" Since Mike was the leadoff hitter, he was already in the on deck circle. He sauntered over to home plate, swinging his bat as he walked. Marilyn pushed through the gate and made a bee line for Mike.

The pitcher went into his stretch. But the umpire saw Marilyn coming and stopped the pitcher and held up his hand as if to say stop. But Marilyn was gathering even more speed. She left the ground some four feet in front of Mike, went fully air born, and came down on his chest. She and Mike fell down on top of the catcher, who fell over backwards and knocked the plate umpire off his feet. A split second after Marilyn tackled Mike, there was a rifle shot. The bullet went just exactly where Mike's head would have been had his mother not brought him and two others to the ground. The bullet lodged in the wooded substructure that was part of the support of the seats behind home plate.

Dennis was as stunned as the rest of the crowd when they saw what Marilyn did. But, before they could react to Marilyn's tackle, they heard the shot. They ducked behind their seats. Some got up and ran for the exit. Others covered babies, small children and some older family members with their bodies. Those who were down on the field ran to the restrooms and the concession stand. Several crawled over the serving counter and fell to safety on the other side. Many were in their cars and trucks in a matter of seconds, creating a horrible bottle neck at the exits to the parking lot. The police officer who got Marilyn to the game on time was directing traffic as best he could, trying to stave off the accidents and injuries that the panic could produce.

Dennis was the lone exception. He did not run away; he ran down to the playing field as fast as he could. He ran to Marilyn and Mike and threw himself over both of them as best he could. The catcher and the plate umpire were still on the ground, holding on to each other, with the umpire clearly on top of the catcher, with his back to center field.

Juan arrived at the ball park just after Marilyn. He noticed a pickup parked down the street, headed in the opposite direction from the ballpark. He also noticed that the parking lot was packed. He made a U turn in the street and went back and parked right behind the pickup parked in the opposite direction. He walked down to the playing field and started his search for Angel. He couldn't find him, and the shot came as he was on the far side of the field from his pickup. He pushed his way through the panicked crowd until he could see the whole playing field. When he looked out into center field and beyond, he saw a man carrying a brief case walking casually toward the pickup he had parked behind. He turned and ran around the back of the stadium, but he was slowed by the hysterical crowd. He finally made it to the street, and from there he could see the man, now running, headed toward his pickup. He broke into a full run himself, still having to work his way through the exiting spectators.

Angel made it to his pickup before Juan could get to him. He jumped in his truck and left with the sound, sight and smell of burning rubber. But Juan could still see his truck when he got to his. He jumped in his own pickup and set out after him.

When Angel left the ball park, he turned left on Ogden Street. He was gaining speed all the time. He then turned right on Avenue F, which put him on Veterans Highway, (377, 277, and US 90 northbound).

It was all that Juan could do to keep Angel in sight. He wasn't losing ground, but he wasn't gaining any either. His siren and lights didn't help all that much. Angel was clearing out the traffic his own way.

Juan was shocked when they came to the Y. He fully expected Angel to continue on 377, 277 into open country where he could drive even faster. But Angel took the left fork, US 90, and headed straight for Lake Amistad. Juan was baffled. Why would Angel take what would eventually be a dead end for him? Then it hit

Juan, Of course, Angel would not want to go deeper into the United States. He would want to get back into Mexico as soon as possible. He could get beyond Juan's jurisdiction. And, even if Juan could follow him back to his hideout, he would be taking on the whole cartel single handedly. Juan mumbled, "I've got to hand it to you Angel, you're not as stupid as you look."

Angel was now actually gaining distance from Juan. Juan could barely see him when he turned off to the right on Spur 454.

"Now what?" Juan mumbled again. "He's going to the boat ramp?" Again, it dawned on Juan what Angel was thinking. "If he can commandeer a boat, he can make it to the international boundary in the middle of the lake before I can get there." But all Juan could do was hope his pickup would gain more speed.

Angel pulled up to the boat ramp, jumped out of his pickup and ran down to the dock. A fisherman, who had a bass boat with a 200 horse power outboard motor on it, was just tying off at the dock. Angel ran up to him, noticed that the keys were still in the ignition, and knocked the man off the dock into the water. He jumped in the boat, started it, backed away from the dock, turned it toward the middle of the lake and pushed the throttle down full force.

Juan could see him leave as he drove into the parking lot. He ran as fast as he could down to the dock. Another fisherman, who had seen what Angel did, and had pulled his fellow fisherman out of the water, recognized Juan, threw him his keys and yelled, "Go get him, Ranger! Use all 250 of those horses!"

Juan jumped in the boat. He too backed it out, turned it and threw it in gear, pushing the throttle down all the way. He was stunned by the power at his disposal.

He soon began to gain on Angel, little by little. But he was gaining.

Angel looked back, and he could see he was losing the race. But there was nothing he could do but what he was already doing.

Juan mused. I wonder if he has a hand gun. That rifle's in a carrying case. He just might be out of luck. I'll watch and wait. When I get a little closer, he'll shoot, if he has anything to shoot.

Juan eased closer. There were no shots. He eased still closer. Angel began to weave back and forth, but it only caused him to lose more space between him and Juan.

They were headed toward the opening into the mouth of the Devil's River. Juan could see the rock cliffs on both sides of the river rising up out of the lake.

Juan pulled his 45 automatic out of his holster. He eased his boat to the right to assure that he would come alongside at the driver's side. When he pulled alongside, Angel turned and looked at him, his eyes filled with hate and fear.

Juan eased over toward Angel's boat as much as he thought he could. Angel was looking straight ahead. Juan raised his gun and took dead aim. Angel turned and looked over at Juan a second time. Juan fired immediately. The bullet hit Angel right between the eyes.

"That's for Hector, you son of a bitch!" Juan said, and smiled the sweet smile of satisfaction. He then pulled his throttle back to neutral, letting his motor idle, and watched. Angel fell forward at a slight right angle on his steering wheel, causing the boat to turn sharply to the right. It was headed for one of the two cliffs at the mouth of the Devil's River. The boat hit the wall going full speed and exploded with the dead Angel and boat debris flying in all directions.

Juan put his 45 automatic back in its holster. He slipped his throttle into forward gear and had a leisurely trip back to the dock. Juan Garza had enjoyed a picture perfect day on Lake Amistad.

Chapter Thirty Eight

"Mom," Mike said as he struggled to get free of his mother's grasp. "You can let me go now. I'm okay."

"I'm sorry, sweetheart," Marilyn responded. "I was just so afraid of losing you."

"So was I," Dennis chimed in.

"Mom, what was this all about? Was somebody really trying to shoot me?"

"Yes."

"Why? I've never done anything to hurt anyone. Why would somebody want to kill me?"

"I know, sweetheart. But these are bad people!"

"What kind of bad people?"

"Bad people who bring dangerous drugs into the United States from Mexico."

"But I don't do drugs."

"No, of course, you don't. We hope you never will, but a lot of people in our country do. The drug dealers make a lot of money selling drugs to them."

"But why shoot me? I'm just a little kid!"

"Mike, you're a very special little kid. You're your grandpa's grandson."

"What does grandpa have to do with it?"

"Mike, these bad people kidnapped your grandpa and took him over into Mexico and told him they wanted to use him as a mule, that's someone who is used to bring illegal drugs across the border."

"Grandpa wouldn't do that."

"This is where you come into the picture. They told your grandpa that, if he didn't do exactly what they told him to do, that they would kill you."

"So grandpa didn't do what they told him to do?"

"No, he didn't. But it nearly cost him his life. He's in the hospital as we speak."

"Earl's in the hospital?" Dennis asked his eyes wide open.

"Yes, Honey. He is, and he's going to be okay, but he's in pretty bad shape now."

"What does bad shape mean?"

"It means he suffered a severe concussion and some cracked ribs and cuts and bruises."

"How did that happen?"

"It happened when he drove his Denali full speed into "Padre Grande.""

"Padre Grande?" Mike said, his eyes getting big. "Are you talking about that huge Mesquite tree out on the Brackettville highway?"

"That's the one."

"Why did he do that?"

"Because he knew that the drug dealers would kill him anyway when the delivery was made."

"Was there anyone with him when he hit "Padre Grande?""

"A drug dealer was behind grandpa's seat, holding a gun to the back of his head."

"What happened to the drug dealer?"

"The collision with "Padre Grande" killed him."

"Brilliant!" Mike exclaimed. "Earl came up with a plan that was high risk, but it was the only way he could save his life, kill the drug dealer and stop the shipment of the illegal drugs."

Marilyn added, "It was high risk. He could easily have been killed alongside the drug dealer. But he took a big chance and won."

"He won," Dennis said, "Because he had a seat belt and an air bag, and the drug dealer didn't even have a seat, much less a seat belt. He had no air bag."

"That's all true, Dennis, but you leave out one critical component."

"What's that, Honey?" Dennis asked in all innocence.

"God," Marilyn responded. Dad came up with a brilliant plan, sure, but, more than that, he put his fate in God's hands."

"Wow!" Mike hollered. "This is right out of the movies!" Mike got very quiet.

"What's wrong, sweetheart? Are you okay?"

"Mom, thank you for saving my life!"

Marilyn teared up and said, "You're welcome, Mike. But your grandpa is the one who really saved your life. He told me in the hospital, when he came to, that someone would try to kill you today."

"How did he know that?"

"I guess you could say he didn't. But he knew the drug dealers well enough by now that he expected them to take revenge on him by killing you."

"I'm going to thank him, too, when I see him."

"That would be very nice, Mike. I know it would mean a lot to him."

"Mom, you could have been killed!"

"I knew that, but I never really thought about it."

"Why?"

Marilyn began to tear up even more, "Because your dad, grandpa, grandma and I love you more that anyone or anything else in the world. That's why."

"Ma'am, here are your car keys," Officer Garcia said, handing the keys to Marilyn.

"Your car is parked on the street just outside the main entrance."

"Oh, I completely forgot," Marilyn said, bouncing her right palm off her forehead. "Thank you so much. And, while we're talking about saving Mike's life, you two need to know that I would never have made it here in time without this wonderful policeman. He took me on the ride of my life through Del Rio. We made it, not a second too soon."

"Thank you, thank you, thank you," Marilyn said and gave him a big hug.

Manuel Garcia blushed and said, "You're welcome. I'm just glad I could help in some small way."

"Correction!" Marilyn said, "You helped in a big way!"

Manuel smiled and excused himself.

Dennis now had tears running down his face. "I could have lost both of you!"

"No, Marilyn corrected again. "You could have lost three of us."

Dennis put his arms around Marilyn and Mike and said, "I've always thought I was the luckiest guy in the world. Now I know I am."

Mike said, "Dad, I think we're all very lucky."

"Oh no!" Marilyn said, putting her hands over her mouth. "I haven't called Mom yet. She'll be a basket case by now! I better do that right now!"

Dennis said, "Let her wait just another minute or two."

"Why? Marilyn said.

"Because, I want to kiss the bravest woman in the world!" He said and grabbed Marilyn and gave her a prolonged kiss.

"Better be careful, Dad," Mike said. She's pretty tough. She just tackled me and knocked me and Tommy and the umpire into the middle of next week. I've never been tackled that hard!"

Marilyn blushed and said, "Men! All you ever think of is football!"

"Hello," Midge said, with more than a little anxiety in her voice.

"Mom," I am so sorry I haven't called you before now, but it's just been crazy out here."

"Sweetheart, just answer one question for me. Is Mike okay?"

"Yes, Ma'am, he's more than okay. He's safe and sound and wonderful."

"Then there was no shooter?"

"Oh, there was a shooter alright."

"But he missed?"

"He did, Mom. I'll tell you all about it when we get to the hospital."

"I am so relieved. Thank God! Drive carefully, Honey, we've had enough excitement for one day."

"I agree. We'll see you in a little while."

Chapter Thirty Nine

"Mrs. Reynolds?"

"Yes, I'm Midge Reynolds."

"This is for Padre," the nurse said and handed Midge a beautiful arrangement of red and white roses.

"Oh my goodness!" Midge said and accepted.

"Look at the card," the nurse said.

"Midge took the lovely card and read: "To our hero, Padre, with love and admiration," and it was signed: The Staff, Val Verde Regional Medical Center.

Midge teared up again. "This is so sweet of you all. Earl, Padre, will be thrilled. Please tell me, what is your name?"

"I'm Judy Gardner."

"Judy, I'm so pleased to meet you. Please express our thanks to everyone."

"I will," Judy said, patted Midge on the shoulder and said, "You're in our prayers."

"Thank you, Judy. That means so much."

Judy turned and almost ran into Juan Garza. "Pardon me," she said.

"No problem," Juan said and smiled.

"Hi Juan," Midge said.

"Hello, Mrs., I mean Midge. How is he doing?"

"He's still asleep, and has been since right after you left."

"Do you know what happened at the ball park?"

"I know enough. I know that Mike's okay."

"He is, thanks to Marilyn."

"Marilyn, really?"

"Yes, she didn't tell you?"

"All she told me is that Mike is okay and that the shooter missed."

"That's true, Midge, but it's not the whole story."

"Well, what is the whole story?"

"The shooter, whom we now know was Angel Martinez, a member of the Diablos, as notorious drug cartel, did miss Mike. But he missed only because Marilyn made a flying tackle and knocked Mike down and out of the way. The bullet Angel fired went through right where Mike's head would have been, but it landed in the substructure behind home plate. It really was quite a tackle, Midge. She managed in one motion to take out Mike, the catcher and the umpire, saving all of them at the same time."

"My daughter did that?"

"Yes, Ma'am, she did."

"What about the shooter, Angel what?"

"Angel Martinez. Well, when Angel fired his shot, the crowd panicked. It was pure bedlam. People were ducking behind their seats, running to their cars, climbing over the serving counter at the concession stand and doing whatever it took to get out of the stadium."

"But what did Angel do? Do we need to worry about his trying to shoot Mike again?"

"Angel ran. He got in his pickup, pulled out on Ogden, went up Veterans Highway and took highway 90 toward Amistad. When he got there, he commandeered a boat and took off for Mexico by water."

"You seem to know exactly where he went."

"I do. I followed him in my pickup, and then by boat."

"What happened then?"

"Since the boat that was loaned to me was faster than his, I caught up with him."

"And then what?"

"I shot him right between the eyes."

"Oh!"

Yes, Ma'am. The answer to your second question is that no one will ever have to worry about Angel again."

"Thank you, Juan. I'm sorry you had to kill him. I know that must be hard on you."

"No, Ma'am. Killing Angel made today the happiest day of my life."

"Then I'm happy for you."

"Midge, I was hoping to talk with Padre, but I'm going to let him rest. I'll come back tomorrow. I'm hoping that, since he was kidnapped and held hostage across the border, he can help us locate the hideout of the Diablos."

"I'm sure he will do his best to help."

"I know he will, Midge. You take care, and get some rest yourself. It's been a long day."

"Juan, it's been a long two days."

"Yes, Ma'am, I'll see you tomorrow.

"Juan."

"Yes, Ma'am"

"You get some rest, too."

"Thank you. I will," Juan said and left.

Midge sat down and let her head rest against the wall. She was almost asleep when Dennis, Marilyn and Mike walked into Room 5. She sprang to her feet and hugged Dennis and Marilyn. Then she turned to Mike and began to cry tears of joy.

"Oh, Mike, I don't think I've ever been as glad to see someone as I am to see you now. Are you really alright?"

"I am, grandma, except for being a little sore from the tackle Mom put on me. Have you heard about what she did?"

"I have. But I'd like to hear your version."

"I wish you could have seen her."

Marilyn was a bright red.

"Maybe you will, since I'm sure Mr. McDermott will have it on video. He always starts his video before the game begins. Anyway, I was ready to take the first pitch when I saw Mom running toward me at full speed. And she was moving fast. I didn't know she could run that fast..."

"I didn't either," Marilyn interrupted.

"Well, she must have been a good three or four feet away from me when she jumped. I mean jumped forward. She looked like J. J. Watt of the Houston Texans. There was no way I could get out of the way. She hit me right here, pointing to his chest. And she took me and Tommy Jackson, the Tigers' catcher, and the umpire out all at the same time. We were all piled up in a heap on and around home plate. I'm telling you. I have never been hit that hard in my life. What is really awesome is that the very moment she hit me I heard a rifle shot."

"I'm just glad I got there in time," Marilyn added.

"So am I," Mike said.

"How is Dad doing, Mom?"

"We think he's doing fine, but it's a little hard to tell since he's been asleep almost since you left."

"Can we wake him?" Mike asked.

"Oh, no, honey," Marilyn said. "We need to let him rest."

"Oh, I'm not so sure about that," Midge said. "I don't think it would hurt him to wake up for a few minutes. With all the pain killers they've given him, he'll go back to sleep without any trouble. The challenge is going to be keeping him awake."

"Can I wake him?" Mike asked.

"You can try, Mike. But don't be too disappointed if he doesn't respond."

Mike walked over to Padre's bed. Without knowing it, he followed his grandma's move earlier and took Padre gently by the shoulders and said, "Wake up, Grandpa, it's time to go fishing." Mike looked back at Midge, as if to ask, "What do I do now?" While he was facing Midge, he heard a groan. Mike looked at his grandpa, and he saw his eyes open a little, then more.

Padre was struggling to focus, but he worked at it until he could see Mike standing over him. When he realized it was Mike, he said, "Mike, it really is you, isn't it?"

"Yep" Mike said. "It's me, safe and sound, same as ever."

Padre's eyes filled with tears. "Oh, thank you, Lord, thank you, thank you, thank you!" He then raised his hands and arms as much as all the paraphernalia would let him. Mike responded by reaching down and joining in the gentle hug.

Mike stepped back one step and then said, "Thanks for saving my life, grandpa."

Padre could only smile. He then added, "I believe your mother had a lot to do with saving you, too."

Marilyn jumped into the conversation and said, "I would never have made it to Roosevelt on time if it had not been for Officer Miguel Garcia. He stopped me because I was driving too fast and then, when I told him who I am, he led me to the ball park at 95 miles an hour."

"I know Miguel, Padre said softly.

Dennis spoke up and said, "I don't think I'm the only engineer in the family. That was quite an engineering plan you put in place."

"Thanks, Dennis. But I had a lot of help," Padre responded.

"Who helped you?"

"The good Lord, I figured if he would provide plans for Abraham and Moses, and especially Jesus, he might be willing to come up with one for me."

Dennis said, "But you've got to admit that it was awfully risky."

"Oh, it was, without a doubt. Everything had to fall into place at just the right time. It did, and I had to turn it all over to the Lord. Besides, what did I have to lose? It was the only hope I had."

"Well, it sure worked, to perfection."

"By the way," Dennis, "The plans the good Lord put in place for Abraham, Moses and Jesus were pretty risky, too. But they all worked."

"Now you've gone to preaching," Dennis said.

"True," Padre said. He then looked a little confused and asked, "Whatever happened to Diego?"

"Who's Diego?" Marilyn asked.

"He's the member of the cartel who escorted me across the river," Padre said.

"Oh, so that was his name," Marilyn responded.

"You're saying was his name. I gather he didn't fare as well as I did."

"He died on impact," Dennis said.

Padre got very quiet. "I really am grateful just to be alive," he said in a near whisper.

Mike followed with, "Me, too."

Marilyn gathered the whole family together around Padre's bed and said, "Let's pray together. She voiced the prayer: "Dear God, we thank you with all our hearts for bringing Dad and Mike through this terrible ordeal safely. You are so good. You are so kind. And your love is wonderful. We pray now for Dad. Bring him to a full recovery. We pray in Jesus' name. Amen."

No sooner had Marilyn concluded her prayer than a nurse pulled back the curtain and said, "Okay, guys, let's let our patient get some sleep." They all hugged Padre one more time in silence and left for home

Jerry McDermott went home after the game and edited his brief video. He isolated Marilyn's tackle from start to finish, added the note "Marilyn Duncan saves her son Mike from an assassin's bullet," and put it on U Tube. It went viral immediately.

Chapter Forty

Dennis, Marilyn and Mike arrived at home about 7:00 p.m. There was a car parked in front of their house. They pulled into their driveway and waited to see who would get out of the car.

A young man who didn't look much older than Mike stepped out of his car and walked up the driveway. He smiled broadly, extended his right hand to Dennis and said, "Hi, I'm Cory Billingsley. I'm with the Del Rio News-Herald. Mrs. Duncan, I'm wondering if I could speak with you for just a few minutes.

Marilyn was so tired that she just stood there stunned for a moment or two. She blew out a deep breath and said, "Sure, I guess so, why not?"

Chapter Forty One

Juan Garza was sipping his morning coffee and reading the morning paper. He looked at the headline and chills ran up his spine. The headline read MARILYN DUNCAN SAVES SON IN HEROIC TACKLE. Juan began reading the story, and he nodded his assent as he read the details he had both lived and re-counted yesterday. He was pleased with the coverage until he came to the final paragraph. It read "The Rev. Earl "Padre" Reynolds is now resting comfortably in the Val Verde Regional Medical Center."

Juan couldn't believe his eyes. He folded the newspaper and left it on the breakfast room table. He went to his bathroom, shaved and then dressed for the day. He tucked the newspaper under his arm and left in a brisk walk to his pickup.

He walked in the front door of the Del Rio News-Herald at 8:00 a.m. sharp. Dewayne Carter, the Managing Editor, had arrived for work only minutes earlier. He was browsing over messages left on his desk overnight. Juan walked up to him, his eyes blazing, and said, "God dammit, Dewayne! How the hell could you do something so damn stupid?"

"Juan, good morning, and what are you talking about?"

"What I'm talking about is right here," Juan said, holding up the paper and pointing to the lead story.

"Isn't that a great story? Can you even imagine someone having the courage Marilyn Duncan displayed in spades yesterday?"

"That's not what I'm talking about," Juan said.

"Then what the hell are you talking about?" Dewayne said, showing no little irritation.

Juan put the newspaper down on Dewayne's desk. He spread it out and put his index finger down on the line that read "The Rev. Earl (Padre) Reynolds is now resting comfortably in the Val Verde Regional Medical Center."

"What's wrong with that?" Dewayne asked. "People have a right to know that Padre's going to be alright. He's as much a hero in this situation as Marilyn is."

"Dewayne, the problem is that we are dealing with a vicious drug cartel headed up by a man who is a sociopath, if not a psychopath. Padre has already cost him two of his key men and several million dollars in narcotics. He's the one who was behind the attempt on young Mike Duncan's life. Diablo Guero's not going to stop now until he kills Padre, or dies trying. We're going to be lucky if they don't try to blow up the whole god damn hospital."

"Aw, shit! We never even thought about that. Juan, I'm sorry. I put a cub reporter on the story last night, and I know that's no excuse, but he just treated it like he would a class assignment at Angelo State where he just graduated. I can do a retraction, if that would help."

"Hell, no, that would only make it worse. Then this end of the Rio Grande Valley would go into shock and mourning. Besides, you'd be up to your ass in law suits when the truth came out."

"Well, I sure as hell don't want lawsuits."

"I'm sure you don't."

"Well, is there anything we can do?"

"Just don't print anything else about Padre until I give you the green light."

"Okay, I won't, and I am really sorry we screwed up. What are you going to do?"

"I'm going to go see Chief and see if I can get a guard at Padre's hospital room door 24/7.

"I'm sure he'll be glad to."

"I hope you're right," Juan said and stomped out.

Chapter Forty Two

The phone was ringing again when Dennis said to Marilyn, "Honey, the computer is frozen. It's bloated on emails."

Marilyn answered the thirteenth call. It wasn't even 10:00 a.m. yet. "What do you think, Honey, should we just put it on the answering machine?"

"I wish we could. But we need to keep the line open in case the hospital calls. We think Dad's okay, but we really don't know yet."

The phone rang again. Dennis said, "I'll get this one. Take a break. Have some more coffee."

"You're an angel," Marilyn said and walked into the kitchen.

"Is this the home of Marilyn Duncan?"

"Yes, it is," Dennis replied.

"Thank you. Is Marilyn there?"

"Yes, she is."

"Please hold for Mr. Johnson.".

"Honey, you have a call from a Mr. Johnson."

"I don't know any Mr. Johnson. Take a message."

"I don't think so. I think maybe you better take this one."

"Okay, if you insist."

Marilyn took the receiver and said, "Hello."

A man's voice came on the line and said. "Is this Marilyn?"

"Yes, it is"

"Marilyn, my name is Jerry Johnson, and I own the Dallas Cowboy franchise in the National Football League."

Marilyn turned pale, swallowed hard and said, "Hello, Mr. Johnson, how are you?"

Jerry said, "I think the better question is how are you?"

Marilyn hesitated a moment and said, "I'm fine, Mr. Johnson."

"Marilyn, I saw that tackle you made on U Tube. I was just wondering if you might be interested in playing linebacker for the Cowboys?"

"You have got to be kidding!"

"I am. But I'm not kidding when I tell you that I think you are a marvelous woman and mother. I'm just as proud of you as the rest of our country is."

"Well, thank you, sir. But I just did what any mother would do."

"I don't think so. In the first place, not very many mothers have your speed and the strength to take out three players at one time."

Marilyn giggled. That was a little weird, wasn't it?"

"Not weird Marilyn, awesome! Anyway, I just wanted to congratulate you on your incredible act of courage and thank you for being the person you are."

"Thank you very, very much."

"And, Marilyn, if you want to, you can tell your girl friends that you've been approached by the Dallas Cowboys with view to becoming a linebacker for us."

"I will. You can count on it!"

"Have a great day, Marilyn."

"You too, Mr. Johnson."

Marilyn sat down in the chair at the telephone desk. She was as limp as a wet dish rag.

"Who was that, sweetheart?" Dennis asked as he walked back into the room."

"You're not going to believe it."

"Try me."

"That was Jerry Johnson, owner of the Dallas Cowboys."

"Naw! You're pulling my leg."

"I am not. He was so sweet! He saw my tackle on U Tube. By the way, how did it wind up on U Tube?"

"Jerry McDermott. Remember? Mike said he was videoing the game, even before it started. Sweetheart, that video has gone viral. You are not only a national celebrity, you're an international one as well."

"Oh my goodness, this is just crazy!"

"Yes, it is. And it's just beginning."

Marilyn walked into the kitchen for another cup of coffee, shaking her head in disbelief the whole way.

The telephone rang again. "I'll get it. You need a breather."

"Is this the home of Marilyn Duncan?"

"Yes, it is."

"Is she available to speak on the phone?"

Yes, she is."

"Please hold for the President."

"Marilyn, you've got another one."

"Dennis, I'm too rattled to talk with anyone else now."

"I really think you need to take this one."

"Aw, shoot! Okay."

"Marilyn, may I call you Marilyn?"

"Sure, everyone else does."

"Marilyn, this is Martin Jackson."

Marilyn felt faint, but she managed to say, "Hello, Mr. President."

"Marilyn, I called to tell you how much I admire you for your amazing courage. You are a remarkable woman, not to mention an exceptional athlete. Marilyn, you are and will be for years a role model for women in America and around the world. Thank you so much for making us all proud."

"Thank you, Mr. President. I can't tell you how much this call means to me."

"You're more than welcome. By the way, Margaret and I would love to have you and your family as our guests for dinner in the White House. Do you think we might be able to get on your schedule?"

"Dinner, at the White House! Yes, sir. You just say when, and we'll be there."

"Oh, that's good. I was hoping you would accept. I'll have one of my staff get together with you in the near future. By the way, the trip is on me. I'm going to have to let you go now. I have a meeting with my National Security Council in a few minutes, and they get surly when I'm late. So, goodbye for now."

"Good bye, Mr. President, and thank you for everything."

Marilyn stood motionless for a full minute with her hands on the top of her head.

Chapter Forty Three

"Padre, you know we have some unfinished business, don't you?" Juan said as he took a seat next to Padre's hospital bed.

"I assume you're talking about the Diablos."

"I am. I've been talking with the Mexican government and they're ready to make a run at them."

"What does a run mean?"

"It means that they are ready to send in the Mexican Army. They're willing to do a full scale frontal attack. But there's a big problem."

"What's the problem?"

"They don't know where they are. We're hoping you can help us find them."

"Oh, Juan, I don't know. I was blind folded after we went across the border. I was even blind folded when I went into their house out of Acuna. I was also put in a room that had the windows nailed shut and some kind of black material over them. It was like living in a closet."

"I understand. I know this is a lot to ask of you, but do you have any feel for where you went once you crossed over into Acuna?"

"Okay, I'll give it a try. I tried to keep track of the left and right turns. But all I can really tell you is that they all added up to a gradual turn to the south and east of Acuna. I also remember the roads, not that I could see them, but their surfaces. We left Acuna on paved highway, but we turned off on a caliche road. Then we went over a cattle guard and up a driveway of some kind to the house. My guess at the time was that it was a ranch, and it was probably isolated enough not to bring any attention to the Diablos."

"How far out of Acuna do you think you were?"

"It's hard to say. But my wild guess is that it was not more than ten or twelve miles. It seemed to me that we got there fairly soon after we left Acuna. Does that help?"

"It does, some. But there are a lot of ranches in that area south and east of Acuna. Is there anything else you can think of?"

"Umn. Oh, there is one other thing I remember."

"What is that?"

"When we first got to their hideout, I heard this loud screeching noise. At first, I was so shocked and scared that I didn't recognize it. Then I remembered that I had heard that same sound when Midge and I were on an anniversary trip to Hawaii. I was playing golf on one of those beautiful courses, and I heard that sound. It scared me half to death, but it turned out just to be peacocks."

"Bingo! Juan said, and jumped straight up out of his chair with his arms and hands reaching for the ceiling. Peacocks! Yes. Padre, you were on the Cordova's ranch. They have, or had, a flock of beautiful peacocks, and they were famous for them all over northern Mexico. The name of the ranch is La Paloma."

"But there weren't any Cordovas there, at least as far as I know."

"No, there weren't. Because they disappeared about six months ago, about the same time the Diablos got very active in our area."

"Disappeared? You mean they just vanished into thin air?"

"Yes. No one knows what happened to them."

"I think I do."

"Really?"

"Really. I think they were slaughtered by the Diablos. I think you could find their bodies, or what's left of them, on the ranch."

"How do you know this?"

"I don't know for sure, but I have a very strong hunch."

"Why?"

"Well, when I first arrived at the ranch, Diego, the driver, and the one who died when I hit "Padre Grande", and another man I came to know as Carlos, were trying to intimidate me, and Carlos wanted to kill me because I couldn't pee fast enough to satisfy him. Diego told him he couldn't because they would have to go get the front end loader and haul me off to the canyon and dump me. He said, it was just too hot to go to all that trouble. My hunch, Juan, is that if a crew went down into that canyon, they would find the remains of the Cordova family."

"Incredible! I feel like a kid on Christmas morning who just found the last piece of the Christmas puzzle. We've got those bastards in our cross hairs, thanks to you."

"I hope so."

"Another subject," Juan said. "Are you up to it?"

"Sure. I haven't done anything since I've been here but eat and sleep."

"Okay. I have another challenge for us."

"And that is?"

"Your safety"

"Juan, I feel safer right here in the hospital than I have in what seems like a long time."

"I'm glad you feel safe. But, you're not."

"I'm not?" Padre said, his eyes getting bigger all the time.

"No, you're not. And you won't be until we take out the Diablos, especially Diablo Guero."

"Oh?" Padre responded.

Padre, you must understand that Diablo Guero is a sociopath or a psychopath, or some combination, and you have cut him to the quick."

"Me? How?"

"Well, for openers, you have cost him his top two henchmen. You have also cost him several million dollars in his failed drug shipment. He's not going to take it lying down."

"You're saying two henchmen. I'm only aware of one, Diego."

"When you crashed, killing Diego and disrupting the shipment, he sent Angel to kill your grandson. To make a long story short, Marilyn saved Mike, and I killed Angel."

"You did?"

"Yes, I did. I chased him on the highway and by boat. I finally caught up with him on Amistad. And I put a bullet right between his eyes."

"Right between his eyes?"

Yes. Why do ask?"

"Because, when Diablo was intimidating me, and he did, he asked Angel if he thought he could hit Mike at the baseball game, and Angel bragged about how he could shoot him right between the eyes."

"Well, chalk one up to poetic justice."

"Amen! But you don't think Diablo Guero believes I'm dead?"

"He did until those idiots down at the News-Herald ran a front page story that wound up by telling the whole g damn world that you are resting comfortably in the hospital."

"Oh, I see what you mean."

"Padre, Diablo Guero is coming after you. You can count on it."

"What about my family?"

"Your family is safe until you go home. Then they could easily become collateral damage. You need to stay in the hospital until we can get some resolution on the Diablos."

"But I can't stay here indefinitely!"

"I know, and you won't have to."

"Are you sure about that?"

"I am. I am also sure that we must move on the cartel as soon as possible. They're in a bit of a state of disarray now, but it won't last. Diablo Guero will not tolerate it. He's a perfectionist and the most obsessive kind. He won't tolerate anything less than perfection. The problem is that you not only have cost him two of his best men and lots of money, you've also embarrassed him. He can't stand that. He's going to kill you or die trying."

"I'd prefer the latter."

"Okay, so here's what we do. We get the Mexican Army in high gear. I can do that faster than you think. Once I tell them that I know where the Diablos are, they will be all over them. In the meantime, we take all the precautions available to us to keep you safe in the hospital."

"What kinds of precautions?"

"Well, at first I thought it might be enough just to post a policeman outside your room door. You're probably not going to be in ICU much longer. But I have a better plan now."

"A plan? That sounds familiar."

"Yes, and it is good one. I guarantee it."

"And what if it doesn't work?"

"The weather is a little warm for May, don't you think?"

"I see. You are going to keep it under wraps until the right time."

"Very good, my friend. Very good!"

"Juan, I'm going to trust you on this. Besides, ignorance is bliss, and I haven't had any bliss in a good while. But I do have two requests."

"Shoot! Whoops, I mean go ahead. What are your two requests?"

"Well, the first one has to do with a young woman I met while in captivity. She was and still is a prisoner of the cartel. She works as a servant in the kitchen. She brought me my lunch just before I left to come back across. But she wasn't brought to La Paloma just to work in the kitchen. She is a sex slave to Diablo Guero."

"Oh!" Juan groaned. I'm sorry to hear that."

"Juan, she is one of those young women who is just too pretty for her own good. She also is wearing an engagement ring. I want the Mexican military to take out the cartel, but I want Maria, that's her name, saved. There could be other innocent people there who are being held against their will. That's my first request."

"And the second?"

"Assuming that the Mexican military is successful, and that remains to be seen, I want you to make a request to the commanding officer to explore the canyon I told you about and see if the remains of the Cordova family can be recovered. I may just be dreaming, but I can visualize a time when we could have a memorial service for them right there on their ranch."

"Padre, your two requests are not only reasonable, but very compassionate. I will present both of them for you."

"Thanks, Juan. It will take a load off my mind, especially my worry about Maria."

"I understand.

Chapter Forty Four

"You have got to be kidding me! You're telling me that that crazy old son of a bitch lived through that crash and is in the hospital in Del Rio?"

Carlos handed Diablo Guero a copy of the morning News-Herald and said, "You can read it all right here. See, down toward the end, he is resting comfortably in the hospital. I don't see how he could have survived either, but the fact of the matter is that he did."

"That old bastard is lying up there in that hospital with good looking nurses all over him laughing his ass off at us, at me!"

"He is alive, Diablo Guero. What are you going to do about it?"

"Kill him, of course!"

Diablo Guero walked around in a large circle, scratching his head, for what seemed like eternity to Carlos, and then said, "I have a plan. I want you to go to the hospital tomorrow. I want you dressed as you would if you were working for a retail merchant. You know, neat and clean, nice shirt and slacks. You will go first to a florist and buy a very nice flower arrangement in a glass vase. You will get a card and sign it 'From your friends in Acuna.' When you get to the hospital, ask the person at the check in desk for the room number for Padre Reynolds. Go to the room. Do not knock on the door. Push the door open very quietly and see if he has any company. If someone says, 'we didn't hear you knock,' you say,' Oh, I'm sorry. I didn't want to wake the patient.' Give the flowers to the person in the room and leave. Repeat this during the day until you find him alone and asleep. When you do, you will very quietly go to his bed and stab him through the heart. You will leave the flowers and exit as quietly as you can. If anyone notices you, smile sweetly and keep moving. Walk out at your normal rate of speed. Remember. You may have to make several trips to the flower shop and the hospital. But, eventually, very likely in the afternoon when he is sleeping, you will have your golden opportunity. It is very important that you not say or do anything that will call attention to yourself or suggest that something is wrong in his room. Do you understand?"

"I do. What you have given me is a beautiful plan. I see no reason why I cannot carry it out to our satisfaction," Carlos said, feeling giddy in his new more important role in the cartel.

"The flower shops may not open until nine or even ten o'clock in the morning. But you need to be there when they open. Often, patients in hospitals take a mid to late morning nap."

"I understand. Thank you, Diablo Guero, for this opportunity to prove myself to you. I will not let you down."

"I know you won't, Carlos. You've been ready to make a move up for a good while now. The only reason you didn't was that you had Diego ahead of you, and he was very good at carrying out special assignments."

"I know. I miss him. He was a good friend."

"He was indeed. Get a good night's rest. You have a big day ahead of you tomorrow."

"I will."

Chapter Forty Five

"You want to do what? Did I hear you correctly? You want us to move Padre up to an isolation room on the third floor so you can lie disguised in the bed in his room, waiting for a drug dealer carrying flowers to come in so you can shoot him? Are you out of your mind?"

"Bob, I know it sounds a little strange…"

"A little! god damn, Juan, this is the craziest scheme I ever heard of. It's got more problems than a run over snake!"

"Well, there are a few things we need to take care of to make it work."

"A few? I guess so. Like giving out a room number for Padre that isn't really his room number, and like having flowers delivered to the room all day by innocent people. What do you plan to do? Shoot everyone who walks in with a vase of flowers, like, if you shoot all of them, you're bound to kill the drug dealer eventually, and like what do we tell Padre's family? Do we tell them we have a room for him, but he's not in it because our security is so bad that we had to put him in isolation? Hell, Juan, he just got out of isolation! This is insane!"

"Bob, please, hear me out on this. I won't take much more of your time."

"It's not my time I'm worried about. It's my blood pressure. I can already tell it's up about twenty points. But, since you're my friend, and, since I have a very deep respect for you as a professional, I will listen. But I'm telling you, friend, you've got a hell of a selling job to do."

"That's fair enough," Juan said. I know the problems you just outlined to me seem impossible to solve, but they're not. I will come back to them a little later and deal with them one at a time. For now, let me broaden the conversation by telling you a little about what we're up against.

You and I are dealing with one of the most vicious drug cartels in the world. Their leader is a man by the name of Diablo Guero. Some call him a sociopath. Personally, I think he's a psychopath. His brutality knows no boundaries or restraints.

Padre Reynolds, by his genius and his courage, has already accounted for the deaths of two of Diablo Guero's key men. And he has disrupted a drug shipment worth several million dollars. Most significantly, he has embarrassed Diablo Guero.

Diablo is determined to kill Padre. He will do it, even if it means burning down this hospital or blowing up half of Del Rio. He will not stop until Padre is dead. Because Padre is in your hospital, the problem is not just mine, it is yours as well. The Diablos are going to make a move here. I believe it will be tomorrow."

"Why tomorrow?"

"Because it is as soon as they can get their plan together. Diablo Guero didn't actually get a confirmation on the loss of his second henchman until this morning's News-Herald. By the way, that story also told him that Padre is resting comfortably in the hospital, meaning your hospital.

Now, let me tell you something that must remain between us. I have been working with the Mexican military. They are planning to surround the hideout where the Diablos are staying tomorrow night. When the dawn comes, they will have their compound completely encircled. Bob, I promise you this. After sunrise, day after tomorrow, the Diablos will just be a bad memory."

"Wow!"

"So we have only one day to deal with, but make no mistake, the Diablos will pay you a visit tomorrow. We have to deal with them here. If we send Padre home, then we put his entire family and home in jeopardy. In other words, Bob, we have to contain and minimize the risk."

"I'm beginning to get the picture."

"Thank you. Now, about those problems you surfaced. They're all real. I have no quarrel with you. Everyone is a sticky wicket. But they're solvable, if we want to solve them. If we don't want to, they are impossible to solve."

"Okay, let's talk about solving them."

"Good. Let's take the matter of Padre's room number. Bob, your staff is savvy enough to know that we need to do this just to increase security. They also know that we have to have a place for delivered flowers. We're already up to our ass in flowers in ICU. Bob, Padre is a legend here. He's not only a hero. He's virtually a saint. This flower thing is going on for a long time. So it will be nice to have a room where they can be collected. As for the family, I'll be glad to talk with them and make sure they know what we are doing and why. Secondly, let's talk about the danger to innocent people. Bob, the only person who is going to be at risk is me. I'm not going to shoot an innocent person. I'm only going to shoot the person who comes at me with a knife or a gun. I'll do it with a silencer on my gun. I can't make it noise free, but I can hold it down. With the door closed, it won't be all that bad."

"You're willing to lie there in that bed and wait until someone comes at you with a knife or a gun?"

"Yes, sir, I am."

"Damn!"

"No one is going to think your security is bad. In fact, I think they'll commend you for taking extra precautions. In other words, my friend, you're not going to look bad; you're going to look good.

Padre could actually stand a little isolation now. The last thing he needs is to be holding open house in his room. He's been through hell, and he is physically, mentally and spiritually exhausted. There is probably nothing in this world that would help him more than long periods of uninterrupted sleep. It will certainly help him prepare for the company he will receive when he gets into a regular room. So what do you think, Bob? Are you ready to take a step or two out of the box and do something that, as risky as it might seem at first, is workable and profoundly worthwhile?"

Bob was speechless. He just nodded in agreement. Finally he said, "Okay, let's get started putting this plan in place."

"Thank you, Bob. You won't regret it."

"I hope not."

Juan left Bob Garfield's office and breathed a huge sigh of relief as he walked down the hall.

Chapter Forty Six

Juan looked like something out of a really bad horror movie. The nurses, whom he was now affectionately calling his make-up artists had him looking just a little better than a mummy. He had bumps and bruises on his head and neck, but most of his recognizable features were covered with bandages. His head didn't look at all like it belonged to the rest of his body. But when he crawled into the bed and pulled the sheets and cover up around him, he looked every bit the part of a seriously injured patient. The nurses stepped back, looked him over, and smiled with pride in their work. He was ready.

Chapter Forty Seven

Carlos stepped out of the elevator and walked down the hall, flashing a big toothy grin. He was carrying a beautiful white vase with a wide variety of blooming flowers. Several of the nurses commented on how pretty it was. He just smiled and kept on walking .When he came to Room 247, he stopped and read the name plate. The patient was listed with a one word designation: Padre. He pushed the door open slowly and as gently as he could. He tip toed in and pulled the door shut behind him. The room was lighted only with the bathroom light that shown through a partially open door. He stood still for a moment or two, trying to adjust his eyes to the near darkness.

When he could see to his satisfaction, he placed the vase of flowers down on the floor near the closed door. He squinted as he looked at the patient. He could see bandages covering his face, and he could make out the shape of his body lying under the sheets. He could tell that Padre was lying on his back.

He mused as he watched Padre for any sound or movement. This is too good! I can stab him right through the heart, and we'll be through with him for good.

He reached down, raised his trousers on his right leg, exposing a long leather sheath. He held the trouser leg up and lifted the large hunting knife from the sheath. He raised the knife high and behind his right ear and took a step forward. By the time he had taken the one step, Padre's double, Juan, all in one motion, had raised up in the bed to a sitting position, thrown the sheets aside and fired four shots into Carlos. The shots seemed to work their way down. The first was between the eyes. The second hit the throat. The third penetrated the chest at the heart and the fourth entered his abdomen.

The impact of successive shots threw Carlos backward. He stumbled over the vase of flowers as he staggered back. He hit the wall and slid down into a sitting position. The flowers were scattered around his feet and legs.

The door to Room 247 flew open. Elaine Davis, the Charge Nurse, rushed in, stumbled over Carlos' body, got up, gathered herself, and said, "Juan, are you alright?"

"Never better," Juan answered, as he crawled out of bed and began picking at the bandages that adorned his face.

"Here," Elaine said, smiling. "Let me help you. We don't want you to hurt yourself."

The patients on both sides of Room 247 hit their call buttons at the same time. When the nurses responded, their question was the same. "What was that?"

One nurse responded to each room. On cue, they said, very casually, "Oh, that noise?"

"Yes, that noise. What was it?"

"Oh, that was just a little electrical hiccup. But it's all taken care of now. No reason to be alarmed. Maintenance has taken care of it. It's not likely to happen again." They concluded with a reassuring smile.

Chapter Forty Eight

Captain Enrique Hernandez stopped his troop convoy just short of the cattle guard on the driveway leading up to the ranch house at La Paloma. He and Lieutenant Jose Ramirez had twenty infantry men at their disposal. Captain Hernandez gathered his men into formation and said, "My orders are for you to encircle the house, but make sure that you have adequate cover. No one needs to be a hero today. There is no reason for you to take any unnecessary risks. We have plenty of ammunition and plenty of time. If necessary, we will just wear them down and run them out of ammunition. We are prepared to stay as long as it takes. I will use the bull horn and give them an opportunity to surrender. If they do, we will simply take them prisoners, hand cuff them and put them in the truck. If they are unwilling to give themselves up, I will order you to begin firing. Concentrate on the windows. If any of them tries to escape from the house, shoot him. Don't try to take anyone prisoner. They are just too dangerous, and we don't want to fall victim to any of their tricks."

"Sir," Sergeant. Garcia said. "I have a question."

"Yes, Sergeant, what is your question?"

"Sir, if they don't surrender, why can't we go ahead and use the rockets? Are we trying to save the house?"

"Good question, Sergeant. No, we're not trying to save the house. But we have been advised that there is at least one innocent in the house."

"Oh, I see. No more questions, sir."

"Any other questions?

"No?"

"Move in and take your positions. Stay alert. We will wait until daylight to make our move."

"Yes, sir" they all said in concert and began to deploy.

A rooster announced that dawn was not far off. Captain Rodriguez looked over at Lieutenant Ramirez and said, "It won't be long now."

The first lights to come on were in the back of the house on the right side.

"Kitchen," Lieutenant Ramirez observed.

Thirty minutes later other lights began to shine. Finally, the sun made its grand entry. Captain Rodriguez raised his bullhorn.

"This is Captain Rodriguez of the Mexican Infantry. I am advising you now that you are completely surrounded with boots on the ground. It is impossible for you to escape from the house. My men are under orders to shoot anyone who leaves the house now on the spot. Do you hear me? Do you understand?"

There was not a sound from the house.

"If you will give yourselves up now and come out of the house, I will guarantee your safety and a fair trial."

There was still no response.

Captain Rodriguez looked over at Lieutenant Ramirez, and shook his head from side to side.

Lieutenant Ramirez took in the Captain's frustration and said, "Captain. Why don't you put them on the clock? Give them ten minutes, or whatever you think is fair, and, if they don't respond, we'll take that as a no."

"Lieutenant, that is a great idea. I'll do just that."

"This is Captain Rodriguez again. I am going to give you fifteen minutes to decide. If you do not come out with your hands up at the end of that time, I am going to assume that you are not going to take my generous offer."

Silence still prevailed.

Captain Rodriguez looked at his watch. "We'll give them the full fifteen minutes, maybe a minute or two more, but, if we don't get some response by then, hopefully a white flag, we will attack in full force."

Lieutenant Ramirez said, "Sir, that's more than fair."

When the ten minutes expired, and there was still no response, Captain Rodriguez dropped his head to his chest and shook his head from side to side, and said. "I was really hoping we wouldn't have to do this."

Before Captain Rodriguez could give the command, there was the sound of windows breaking and gun shots followed rapidly from assault rifles. Captain Rodriguez and Lieutenant Ramirez retreated behind the closest tree.

"Fire!" Captain Rodriguez yelled into the bull horn. A simultaneous volley of bullets rained in the windows of the ranch house.

"Continue firing!" Captain Rodriguez yelled again into the bull horn. And another burst of thunder rained still more bullets through the windows. His troops kept up their firing until he called a halt. "Cease Firing!" He ordered.

An eerie silence set in over the ranch. It lasted a full five minutes.

"What do you think, Lieutenant?"

"I think they're holding a committee meeting without their leader," Lieutenant Ramirez responded. "Captain, I know these are bad men, but they're not stupid. They know that we can continue firing until hell freezes over. They know they don't really have a chance."

"Damn, Lieutenant. You're right," Captain Rodriguez said, as he took note of the white flag that had emerged from the front door. He quickly got on the bull horn again.

"Put your weapons down, Come out with your hands up, and walk single file down the driveway toward the cattle guard," he ordered.

One by one, four of the Diablos walked through the front door and began their walk down the driveway. When it was obvious that the last one had emerged, Captain Rodriguez turned to Lieutenant Ramirez and said, "I don't see Diablo Guero."

"I don't either," Lieutenant Ramirez said. "He would stand out like a sore thumb."

Captain Rodriguez spoke on the bull horn again, this time to his troops, "Come in and take charge of the prisoners."

When the prisoners were hand cuffed and loaded onto their truck, Captain Rodriguez turned to Lieutenant Ramirez and said, "Lieutenant, I want you to take Garcia and Zuniga and go in and sweep the house. Open every door. Every door! If there is an entrance to the attic, go up and check there. Be very careful. Diablo Guero is in there somewhere, and there may be others. Plus we know that there is at least one innocent in there."

"Yes, sir, Captain, what's going to happen to these prisoners?"

"We'll turn them over to the local authorities, and they will stand trial for the murders of the Cordova family, the people who lived here before the Diablos killed them and stole their ranch."

"Good! I hope they get what's coming to them."

"Don't worry, Lieutenant, they will. They will. I promise you."

Lieutenant nodded his approval and walked over to Garcia and Zuniga.

"Garcia, Zuniga, we're going in," Lieutenant Ramirez said. We're going to bring out Diablo Guero and any more of his henchmen who are in there. Plus we are going to do our best to save some innocent people."

"Yes, sir," the soldiers said in unison.

Lieutenant Ramirez, Sergeant Garcia and Corporal Zuniga walked slowly and quietly through the open front door. Lieutenant Ramirez motioned for Garcia to take the left side of the house, and he moved toward the kitchen. All of them opened every closet door they passed, but no one surfaced. Sergeant Garcia pulled down the drop stairway and checked the attic. No one.

Lieutenant Ramirez walked into the kitchen. He saw that the kitchen had a large walk in pantry. Very slowly he opened the door, taking special precautions to assure that he would not be in the line of any fire.

He looked in; tears filled his eyes. Lupe was on her knees on the floor. She was facing him, and she had her hands together in the tent formation, muttering something to the Virgin Mary. Her eyes were closed, but, when she heard the door open, she looked up and saw Lieutenant Ramirez. She broke into a large smile. She reached out to him. And he helped her get up off the floor. When she was upright and stable, she reached around him and gave him a huge hug. "Bless you! Bless you!" She said. He helped her to a breakfast room chair, all the while holding his index finger over his lips.

When he could see that she was beginning to calm down, he asked her, "Where is Diablo Guero?"

"He is in his big bedroom." She said.

Lieutenant Ramirez whispered "Gracias," kissed her on the head, sat down long enough to remove his combat boots, turned and started walking down the long hall to the master bedroom in his stocking feet.

He walked slowly and cautiously down the long hallway. As he neared the master bed room, he could hear the sounds of a scuffle taking place. He stopped and listened for a moment. The sounds persisted. He eased his way down toward the door. It was open. He discovered that he could look into the room, at least part of it, by looking at the enormous mirror that went from floor to ceiling and extended down a long wall. He was shocked by what he saw.

When he got close enough to get a good look into the mirror, he could see that the struggle was between Diablo Guero and a young woman. He squinted his eyes, and what he saw caused his heart to do flip flops. The young woman was Maria, his Maria, his fiancé Maria. His heart began to pound as never before.

"Dammit! Stand still!" Diablo Guero said. He had her out in front of him, trying to hold her with his left hand and arm while holding a revolver in his right hand. She was wearing the ensemble provided by Diego, and it included a pair of stiletto high heels.

She extended her right leg as far as she could and came back with the stiletto heel as hard as she could. She caught Diablo Guero on his right shin. He screamed in pain, put his gun down on the bed and spun her around. She was now behind Diablo Guero. Lieutenant Ramirez stepped into the open doorway. Maria saw past Diablo Guero just enough to recognize Jose.

"Jose!" she screamed at the top of her lungs. Diablo Guero swung around and went for his gun. But it was too late.

Jose emptied his service revolver into Diablo Guero before he could even reach his gun. Diablo Guero fell into his huge glass mirror. It shattered and made a bed of glass for his landing area.

Maria took one step forward and jumped up into Jose's arms. They stood and hugged and kissed until Sergeant Garcia showed up, looked down at the body of Diablo Guero, cleared his throat twice, and said, "We took Lupe out to the Captain. She's going to be okay, once she gets over being scared to death, then added, with a twinkle in his eye, "Lieutenant, we've opened every door in the house and checked the attic, but I don't mind looking some more if you think I might find a woman as beautiful as Maria."

"You've looked enough, Sergeant."

When Maria, Jose, Sergeant Garcia and Corporal Zuniga reached the front door, Sergeant Garcia called them to a halt.

""I've got an idea."

"Oh?" Jose said skeptically, knowing that Sergeant Garcia always had an idea.

"Yes," he said. "Since you two are engaged, why don't we have some fun with the guys?"

"Like what?" Jose asked cautiously.

"Well," he said. When we walk out the front door, Zuniga and I will go first. We'll walk out shoulder to shoulder. Then you two follow us, you know, just like you were walking out of the church at the end of the wedding?

Maria beamed. "I love it! Let's do it!"

Jose didn't have anything else to say.

Captain Rodriguez and his troops were shocked when they saw Garcia and Zuniga holding hands and skipping down the front walk. A brief pause was followed by uncontrolled laughter.

Jose and Maria emerged from the house. The walked out with Maria's left arm gently nestled into the crook of Jose's right arm. They weren't skipping like the two bridesmaids before them, but they were walking at a good clip.

The "congregation" broke into a boisterous applause that was a mixture of hand clapping and shouts of joy.

When the noise subsided, one of the troops standing next to Captain Rodriguez said, "Hey, Captain. What do you think about that?"

Captain Rodriguez smiled broadly and began singing "Here Comes the Bride." His troops gleefully joined him. The music was terrible, but the thought was superb.

Chapter Forty Nine

"I really appreciate the invitation to be on your show, but I'm going to have to decline. My family has been through a lot lately, and I think my place is here with them. But I appreciate your call, and I wish you well with your show."

"I understand."

"Thanks for understanding."

Dennis asked Marilyn, "Who was that?"

"That was another talk show invitation. Speaking of talk shows, have you ever heard of a talk show called 'Dave Digs It?'"

"I can't say that I have. But then I don't watch talk shows anyway. I'm glad you're turning them down. Honey, the truth is that they need you a lot more than you need them."

"I know. But what I told him is the truth. I just have this feeling way down deep that we need to stay pretty close to home for a while. I think we've had about all the excitement we can enjoy for now."

"Oh, I agree. It's a little hard to explain to people, but I am also feeling the need to have all of us close by. I think maybe it's rooted in our need to know that we're all safe."

"Sweetheart, I couldn't agree more."

"Oh, I almost forgot. Bill Anderson gave me a couple of pieces out of the New York Times. Did you know you made the New York Times?"

"No, really? What did he give you?"

"Well, the first one is this cartoon," Dennis said, and handed a folded up piece of newsprint to her.

"Oh, my, gosh!" she yelled. "I can't believe this!" But she stood in awe as she looked at a cartoon that depicted Captain Marilyn flying over the White House with her cape unfurled behind her. The caption below the picture read 'Marilyn for President.' She handed the piece of newsprint back to Dennis and said, "Honey, this is insane."

"It is," he said, "But it's really funny too."

"Okay. What else did Bill give you?"

"Well, this one is definitely not a cartoon. It is an article by David Brown. Sit down. You may want to read this slowly."

Dennis handed Marilyn a much larger piece of folded newsprint, and they sat down.

Marilyn opened it and began to read. The headline read "Marilyn Duncan: A Woman of Courage."

The text read as follows: "Marilyn Duncan of Del, Rio, Texas is a woman of courage. This week, in a spontaneous act of undeniable courage, she threw herself into her twelve year old son Mike, the leadoff hitter in a Little League baseball game, the catcher from the opposing team, and the umpire to shield Mike from an assassin's bullet. She was successful, but only by a fraction of a second. Any later, Mike would have been shot, by the best estimates of police experts, right between the eyes. In tackling Mike, she also took the catcher and the umpire out of harm's way.

Did Marilyn wake up that morning feeling courageous? I doubt it. I doubt if very many of us walk around feeling courageous. I have serious doubts about the folk notion that courage is a virtue. I don't think we know very much about our courage until we are presented with an obvious situation which calls for it. Then we find out very quickly whether or not we have courage.

America prides itself on being 'The land of the free and the home of the brave.' I believe this is true. I am also hopeful enough to believe that it will always be true. But, as I did with courage, I will ask about bravery. Who are the brave?

I believe the brave are those Americans who have shown bravery. We have a proud history as a nation of the sacrifices of young men and women who have demonstrated incredible bravery in some of the real hell holes of the world. But I submit to you that they didn't know just how brave they were until they acted.

In short, what I am asking you to think about is this. If bravery is not a virtue, then what is it? I take the position that bravery is the outcome of a decision.

Marilyn didn't decide to be brave. She decided, and very quickly, without time to vacillate, to do whatever had to be done to save Mike. Marilyn Duncan is an American hero. Why? Because she was able to do what she believed had to be done.

The American military has a long history of doing what has to be done. Courage has been demonstrated a million times over, and bravery has become common among our defenders of our freedoms. We live in awe of our American heroes. This is the way it should be.

I commend the same sequence to our political leaders. Do what needs to be done when it needs to be done, and you will find the courage. You also can join the ranks of our heroes. You can begin by taking a page out of Marilyn's playbook."

Marilyn was in tears. Dennis reached out and pulled her into his chest. He said, "Honey, everything the man wrote is true. Thanks for being you."

Chapter Fifty

"Padre," the nurse said, as she tapped and peeked into his room. "You have some guests."

Padre sat up straight in bed, laid the morning "News-Herald" aside, ran his right hand over his hair, and said, "Well, let them in. Let's see who they are."

Jose opened the door and waited for Maria to clear before he closed it. When she was in the room, he took her hand again.

"Maria! Maria!" Padre shouted. "Thank God, you're safe. Now I can get a good night's sleep. I have been worried sick about you. I just couldn't do anything to help you!"

"But you did! Padre, we know the story. Everybody knows the story. You came up with a plan that saved you and your grandson. You also saved me! The Mexican soldiers who rescued me would never have known where to find me if you had not told them how to find the Diablos. And, guess what, Padre?"

"What? Please tell me."

"Jose, Lieutenant Jose Ramirez, is the one who saved me from Diablo Guero. Padre, I want you to meet my fiancé, Jose, Lieutenant Jose Ramirez."

"Your fiancé?" Padre said in amazement. "Then you," Padre said, pointing to Jose, "You are the young Lieutenant who shot and killed Diablo Guero?"

"I am, Padre, and, I'm sorry, but I must tell you, in all honesty, that it was a real pleasure."

"Jose, I'd be a hypocrite if I told you anything other than that I am very glad that Diablo Guero is dead. My goodness! So the engagement ring I saw you wearing, Maria, came from Jose?"

"Yes, it did. The only reason I got to keep it on was that Diego loved to make a joke and tell everyone at La Paloma that I was engaged to him."

"Oh, sweetheart, what you've been through!" Padre said as he shook his head.

"But she was very brave, Padre. When I found her, she was fighting him with all her strength. In fact, she kicked him with the heel of her shoe, a stiletto high heel, and made him lose his grip on her and turn around toward me. You've probably figured out already that he was going to use her as a human shield."

"I'm not surprised. Nothing that man could or would do would surprise me," Padre said and added, "Isn't it interesting that a man with that much bravado would hide behind a woman when the chips were down?"

"He was a coward, Padre." Jose responded.

"He was, and a very evil and dangerous one," Padre agreed. "How are you feeling?"

"I'm doing fine. The doctor told me yesterday that, if I continued to do as well as I've been doing, he'll let me go home sometime today. But he hasn't made his rounds yet. So I am just waiting."

"I'll bet you're more than ready, true?"

"Oh, I've been ready for a good while. But we had to deal with a little complication named Carlos before I could move to this room."

"Carlos? The Carlos of the Diablos?" Maria asked.

"Yes, that Carlos, Maria. Diablo Guero sent him to the hospital to kill me, but Texas Ranger Juan Garza killed him."

"Wow!" Maria said, her eyes getting bigger and bigger.

"Maria, you may not know that Juan also killed Angel."

"I guessed that something like that happened. We know the story about how your daughter saved her son from an assassin's bullet, and we assumed that the assassin was probably Angel, but we never heard what happened to Angel. What happened?"

Juan chased him clear out to Amistad, and then chased him again in a boat about half way across the lake before he caught up with him and killed him."

"I'm glad he's dead. He was a blood thirsty killer!"

"He was indeed. Good riddance."

"Padre," Jose said, shifting from one foot to the other and back, "There's something we'd like to ask you."

Jose paused for a moment.

"Well, go ahead and ask him!" Maria said, her impatience on display.

"Padre, we are ready to get married, and we were hoping you'd marry us, since you are a minister and all."

Padre lighted up with a big smile. "Of course, I'd be honored to marry you two."

"Well, we know you need some time to get your strength back, so we were thinking about maybe about June 15."

"My answer is yes. Of course, I would love to officiate at your wedding." Padre grinned and said, "That'll also give me some incentive to get well sooner. June 15 is only three weeks away."

"We know, and we're sorry, but we've already been waiting a long time, and, well, we are so ready…"

"I know," Padre said. "This is not my first rodeo; I mean wedding. I've also seen a lot of weddings moved up and very few postponed. Don't worry. We'll do it. It'll all work out."

Jose and Maria turned to each other. Both were beaming. They turned back to Padre and Jose said, "Oh, thank you!" Jose shook Padre's hand vigorously. Maria leaned over and gave him a kiss on the cheek.

"Hey, you two, time's up. Let's give our patient some rest," a nurse said as she held the door open for the excited couple.

"Yeah," Padre said. "I'm going to need it. I'm doing a wedding, a very important wedding."

Chapter Fifty One

"Good to see you, Juan. I understand you've been busy," Padre said as Juan tapped on the door and walked into his room.

"I have been busy, but I like it that way. I didn't become a ranger just to sit around and wait for something to happen."

"Well, my friend, you haven't had to wait long lately. What's going on?"

"Let me ask you a question first. How are you doing? Do you think you'll be going home any time soon?"

"Juan, I'm doing great. The doctor tells me my ribs are healing nicely, and I haven't had this much rest in as long as I can remember. I'm still a little weak, but I think that's just from inactivity. As soon as I get out of here, I'll be able to start some light exercise, and that will help me build up my strength."

"That's well and good, but don't push it. You don't want to wind up back in here."

"No, I don't, but I can't imagine being in a better hospital. These folks have treated me like royalty."

"Padre, you may not know it yet, but you are royalty. I've been talking with some of the folks around City Hall, and they are already planning a Padre Reynolds Day for Del Rio and Ciudad Acuna."

"Aw, they don't need to go and do something like that. Why would they do that?"

"Listen, my friend, they are doing it because they love you and because you turned the tables on the Diablos."

"Well, I had a lot of help along the way, or it would never have turned out the way it did. You know that. You yourself were a huge part of our success in getting rid of Diablo Guero and his men."

"Well, you can say whatever you want to when it gets to be your time to talk, but we all know that you are the one who made it all possible."

"That's not quite true, Juan."

"What do you mean?"

"I mean that, without the good Lord's help, I would never have had a plan that would work. But he came through in a big way. Juan, it was just miraculous. Everything had to work in perfect timing. I could never have made that work on my own."

"I hear you. Don't faint when I tell you, I'm going to Mass on Sunday, unless I get called out."

"Wonderful!"

"It may feel a little weird to me at first."

"Why is that?"

"The last time I went to Mass, St. Peter was the priest."

Padre laughed until his ribs hurt, and said, "Maybe my ribs are not quite as healed as I thought."

"I'm sorry. I won't do that again."

"Oh, don't stop. Humor is what keeps us human."

"Padre, I came mainly to see how you are doing, but I also have a report on the Cordova family."

"Oh, good, what have you learned?"

"A company of engineers out of the Mexican Army did a search and dig operation on La Paloma. I told them what you told me about the front end loader and the canyon, so they went south of the house to a good size canyon and began to excavate. It was no time at all before they unearthed five bodies. Padre, they were in bad shape. They were badly decomposed and unidentifiable. But they all had one thing in common. All five had been shot in the back of the head execution style. They could determine that there were three adult bodies and two children. I've talked with people in Acuna who knew the family, and they have told me that there was a grandmother living with Mr. and Mrs. Cordova and their two children, a boy about eight and a little girl five."

Padre bowed his head and mumbled, "O, Lord, how terrible!"

"It is. This kind of thing should never happen in a civilized society."

"Juan, sometimes I wonder just how civilized we really are."

"So do I."

"Is there any extended family?"

"I did talk with the Catholic priest in Acuna this morning, a Father Marquez, and he tells me that Mr. Cordova has a brother who lives in Mexico City. He's a banker. He's been on the phone with the authorities, night and day, since his brother and his family disappeared. I haven't called him yet. I just haven't had time, but I will."

"Juan, when you talk with him, tell him that I would like to do a memorial service at La Paloma for the family. Please give Father Marques another call, and tell him I want him to participate with me. Father Marquez and I are good friends, and I know he'll be glad to participate."

"Padre, are you sure you want to do that service at La Paloma? It got pretty shot up when the army took out Diablo Guero and the few men he had left."

"I know. We'll have to do some work to take care of a good size crowd. The people of Acuna and some others are going to come. They're not only going to be looking for some kind of closure on this horrible nightmare, they are going to want to celebrate the fact that the Diablos no longer own anyone or anything. I know it sounds a little crazy, but, believe me, it will have a healing effect."

"Okay, you're the preacher. We'll do it. I know some guys in Acuna who will come out and help."

"You don't have to make it brand new. What I understand is that most of the windows got shot out. If we could just repair the windows and clean out the inside where glass and debris are bound to be, so we can turn on the air conditioner, it would work as well as anywhere. We'll most likely do the service out in the open air and serve refreshments inside the house for those who want to stay and visit."

"You've been thinking about this, haven't you?"

"Juan, you and I are just alike, with one exception."

"What's that?"

"You've got too much to do, and I've got too little. Yes, I have been thinking about that family and what we might do to bring some comfort to the people who knew and loved them. I think this will go a long way."

"I can't argue with that."

"When you talk with Father Marques, tell him I'll be glad to do the homily. He's more like you than me. He's got too much to do. All of these solo priests who are serving these big parishes do. I've known a lot of them. They're doing a sacrament of some kind every time they turn around. He'll be glad to let me do the homily. Trust me."

"Padre, I've been trusting you for a long time."

"The same goes for me, my good friend."

"Well, I'd better get started. I'll get back with you on a day and time when I get a better hold on all this."

"That's fine. I'll be home soon, and I'll probably get bored in about ten minutes. I'll look forward to your call."

"Sounds like a plan."

"It does sound like a plan, doesn't it? And, Juan, there is one more thing."

"What's that?"

"I'd like to read your job description some time."

Juan laughed and left.

Dr. Jordan, the Charge Nurse and Midge walked in as Juan walked out. He looked at Padre for a moment or two, smiled and said to the Charge Nurse, "He looks good to me. Get him ready, and roll him out."

Chapter Fifty Two

"Padre, I'd like for you to meet Enrique Cordova. He is the brother to the late Mr. Cordova."

"I am very pleased to meet you, Mr. Cordova. I know this is a difficult time for you, and we appreciate your coming. My hope is that the service today will bring you some comfort. Even though I don't know how many people will come today, I know they will want to share the burden of your loss and offer you comfort as well."

"Juan tells me you are known as Padre. May I call you Padre?"

"Oh, please do."

"Will you call me Enrique?"

"Okay, Enrique," Padre said, shaking Enrique's hand vigorously.

"Padre, it is I who need to be expressing gratitude. I am deeply grateful to you and Juan for making this day possible. I don't mean just the service. Juan has told me the story of your kidnapping and escape. Padre, you are a very brave man. You are deeply admired and loved by all the people."

"Thank you, Enrique, for those kind words. But the truth is that I am also a very fortunate man. I give God all the credit for making this day possible. Without his help, things would have never worked out this way."

"I understand. You are a true man of God."

Padre was beginning to blush. "Look," he said, pointing toward the cattle guard. "People are already beginning to arrive. And it's more than an hour before the service."

"Padre, I want to give you a list of my family members. I did not include their full names because, as you know, our Spanish names can get a little long. But I will appreciate your mentioning each one by name."

"I wouldn't have it any other way, Enrique. In fact, I was about to ask you for a list. Thank you."

"Juan, is he always this nice?" Enrique asked.

"Except when he plays golf," Juan laughed. "Then he turns into a cut throat gambler, and he takes no prisoners."

"Juan! Please! Don't ruin everything! I think I had Enrique sold on me."

"Padre," Enrique responded quickly, "I am sold on you 100 per cent. But, tell me. I am very curious about one thing."

"Oh? What's that?"

"Doesn't it bother you to come back to La Paloma? I mean this place where you were held captive and treated so badly?"

"Actually, it hasn't bothered me so far. But this is the first time I ever saw the area around the house. The times when I came and went I was blind folded. So this beautiful park like area is all as new to me as anyone who is coming for the first time. I will go in the house, but not until after the service."

"I think that is a good decision," Enrique agreed.

"Gentlemen, if you will excuse me, I need to visit a moment with Father Marquez. I see him parking his car."

"By all means," Enrique said. "Feel free to do whatever you need to do."

"Father Marquez, It is so good to see you again. Thank you for coming and offering to help me. As usual, I need all the help I can get."

"Padre, I think you do quite well on your own. I am honored to be included in this very special service. I will be glad to lead us in a prayer. Just so you know what is coming, I will not only pray for the people, I will also pray for the house."

"You can do a full blown exorcism, if you want to. There has been enough evil in that lovely home to fill up several lifetimes."

"Well, I won't go quite that far, even though we priests are all ordained to be exorcists, but I will address the situation in my prayer."

"Thank you, sir. It is an honor for all of us to have you here."

"No, Padre, the honor is all mine."

"Father, I need to let you go now. I need to talk with our musician and our reader for a moment."

"Please, do what you need to do. I'll be fine. In fact, I see some of my parishioners coming in now."

Padre visited with the reader, a sixteen year old boy from a neighboring ranch family and a young woman from a Baptist church in Acuna. When everyone was on the same page, he left them and sat down in one of the two folding chairs behind an old and worn pulpit that had been brought in from a storage room at a Pentecostal church in Acuna.

"Padre," a young man from Acuna said, kneeling down to speak in Padre's ear. "We've got two hundred chairs set up, and we don't have any more."

"Then you've done the best you can. Don't worry about it. Some may have brought some folding chairs, and some may just have to stand. The service will not be all that long. We'll be okay. Thanks for your help."

Padre scanned the two hundred chairs. They were full. It was still twenty minutes until the service was scheduled to begin. He didn't know what to do but wait. When the time came for the service to begin, he looked out beyond the two hundred people seated and estimated another two hundred in folding chairs and standing.

An older man seated on the back row turned around and looked at the crowd standing behind him. He saw an older woman with a cane standing on the front row. He immediately got up from his chair and walked back to her. He didn't say a word. He just took her by the arm and led her to his chair where he pointed down. She teared up as she said, "Oh, thank you."

Several other men, young and old, followed suit. They also began to work in those families with small children.

An eerie silence swept over the congregation when the appointed time arrived. All of the talking stopped. Everyone was looking straight ahead at Padre.

Padre stood, stepped up to the pulpit and spoke into a microphone that been supplied by the local volunteer fire department. He smiled and said, "Welcome. Thank you for coming today", then added, "Grace to you and peace from God our Father and the Lord Jesus Christ." He then nodded to the young woman musician.

She walked up to the pulpit, guitar in hand, bowed her head in prayer for a moment and began singing "This is the day the Lord has made." She sang slowly at first, then picked up the pace with a second time through and then invited the congregation to sing by reaching out with her left hand and arm, inviting them both to stand and to sing. The people sang too softly for her. She stopped them. "I can't hear you! Sing! Praise the Lord!" She started again, and this time the people sang at full volume.

Padre stood and said, "Thank you, Miranda. You know, I should have started doing that a long time ago."

There was sympathetic laughter.

Padre then nodded to the scripture reader. He rose, came forward and began reading from Psalm 46.

> "God is our refuge and strength, a very present help in trouble. Therefore we will not fear though the earth should change, though the mountains shake in the heart of the sea; though its waters roar and foam. Though the mountains tremble with with its tumult…. The Lord of hosts is with us; the God of Jacob is our refuge."
>
> (Revised Standard Version)

Padre stood and said, "We are here this morning to remember the Rafael Cordova family. Specifically, we remember Rafael, husband and father; we remember Theresa, wife and mother; we remember Consuela, wife, mother and grandmother; we remember Carlos, son and brother, age 8; and we remember Angelita, daughter and sister, age 5. We rejoice that they are now in heaven with their heavenly Father. Never again, will they be afraid. Never again, will they be attacked. Never again, will they be hurt. Never again, will they be killed. Because death itself has been destroyed by the resurrection of our Lord Jesus Christ." He nodded again to Miranda.

She came forward, took her place behind the pulpit and said, "Again, I will sing the song first, and I invite you to join me after that. She gulped, took a deep breath and began singing "Jesus loves me, this I know, for the bible tells me so. Little ones to him belong; they are weak, but he is strong…"

The congregation stood and sang. There was a sea of white handkerchiefs bobbing across the crowd.

Padre wiped his own eyes and stood up again. I want to begin my homily for you this morning with a report of good news. The Diablos cartel has been destroyed. Before he could continue, the congregation rose and applauded for a full minute.

Padre nodded his head up and down and continued. Four of them have been killed, including their notorious leader, Diablo Guero. The other four are now in custody of the authorities and have been indicted on the charge of capital murder for the murders of the Cordova family. My friends, I can assure you that justice will be served."

The congregation rose again and applauded, this time even louder than the first. "Friends, we are a people in mourning. We are a grieving family and community. We have lost loved ones and especially children. There is no sugar coating the pain that we all feel. It is a natural and normal pain. It's okay to cry, no matter how old you are. It hurts!

We can, however, help each other. Tell your stories about the Cordova family. Remember all the good times. Listen carefully to each other, and share the pain. No one need bear this horrible burden alone.

I needed help as I thought about what I might tell you that would be most helpful to you in the future. So I turned to my old friend the Apostle Paul. In particular, what he has to say to us from his letter to the Romans. I'm just going to read a small part of what he has to say, but I commend all of Chapter 12 to you.

Listen to the Word of God:

> "Beloved, never avenge yourselves, but leave it to the wrath of God, for it is written, 'Vengeance is mine, I will repay, says the Lord. No, 'if your enemy is hungry, feed him; if he is thirsty, give him drink; for by so doing you will heap burning coals upon his head.' Do not be overcome by evil, but overcome evil with good." Romans 12:18-21 (RSV)

The first time I read this passage, I really liked that part about heaping coals on his head. I suspect that more than one of us here this morning would like to heap burning coals on the heads of all the Diablos. Wouldn't you? Raise your hand, if you think this is a good idea."

There was a sea of hands going up. Padre was not surprised. He felt their feelings down deep inside himself as well.

"But, wait a minute! What did Paul say first? He said that vengeance is the Lord's, not ours. I told you earlier that justice will be done. But it is a justice that God has assigned to the governing authorities. If you don't believe me, go ahead and read Romans 13. So there are already two conclusions that are obvious.

The first is that vengeance belongs to the Lord. Aren't you glad? I mean really! You can just look at the Diablos to see what happens when people decide they are the ones to mete out vengeance. You don't really want to be like the Diablos!

The second conclusion is a little tricky. But I will summarize. What Paul is telling us in a nutshell is twofold: First, we are not to sink to the level of the Diablos. Second, we are to be just as good as they are bad. In being that good, we bring them to shame. That shame is the burning coals Paul is writing about.

God and Paul have gone to a lot of trouble, my friends, to try to make it clear to us that the high road is the only road to take. It is the only road that will free us from hate, bitterness and a distorted sense of what is right and wrong.

We simply cannot let the Diablos' kind of people take over the world. If we do, goodness will vanish and human life won't be worth living. We can resist them, as we have done. We can turn them over to the authorities, as we have done. But we must stop short of letting anger make us like they are.

The Diablos are no longer a threat to us. They can't hurt us anymore. Unless we let hate for them change us into hate filled people. That will hurt us more than anyone else.

I have one footnote to add. Some will say that we are here today to bring closure to this tragedy. That is only true in a very limited way. Yes, we are here to celebrate the fall of the Diablos, an end to their reign of terror. There is some sense of closure in that. But there is no such thing as closure on the experience our loved ones and we have experienced. Nor does it make sense to talk about forgive and forget. Forgive? Yes.

Forget? No! It's impossible. But it is possible and profoundly worthwhile to pursue goodness. The goodness that is rooted in the Holy Spirit's working through the medium of time will lessen the pain and enrich the memories. God bless us all! Glory be to the Father, and to the Son and to the Holy Spirit. Amen."

As Padre sat down, the congregation rose to a standing ovation. He blushed again.

Father Marquez stepped up to the microphone. "Let us pray," he said in a deep and vibrant voice.

"Our Father, we come before you with heavy hearts. We have lost loved ones near and dear to us. We come now remembering them. We give thanks for every member of the Cordova family. We thank you for Rafael. We thank you for his love for you and his family. We thank you for his faithfulness to his wife Theresa and for their love for each other and their children. We thank you for Theresa's skillful parenting that made each child feel special. We thank you for Consuela, who brought to the family a great gentleness and the wisdom of the ages. We thank you for Carlos, whose enthusiasm for life was so contagious. We thank you that he was a good big brother for Angelita, 'Our little Angel', as the family knew her. We thank you for all that was good and innocent in her. We thank you that she loved life so much that she couldn't stop singing. Help us, our Father, to remember with clarity and grace. We thank you, O Lord, that these loved ones are loved most by you. And we thank you that they have now been received into the places promised for them by our Lord Jesus Christ.

Lord, we pray for this place. We know it has also been victimized by the presence of terrible evil. We pray now, in the name of Jesus, that you will exorcise it of all evil. Cleanse it and renew it for new life.

We pray especially for the house. We pray that it may be transformed by your miraculous powers from a place of darkness to a place of light. Purge it, we pray, from every vestige of the evil that has ruled it.

We pray now that the house may again become a place where love prevails, where children are safe, where good memories are made, where old memories can be cherished, where love is nurtured by laughter, where mistakes are seen as trivial, not fatal, where hospitality has replaced hostility, and, most of all, where you, not a godless one, is the head of the family.

We offer all of our prayers in the name of Jesus, through whom we have life in its fullness and in eternity. Amen"

Father Marquez returned to his seat. There was total silence.

Padre nodded again to Miranda. She returned to the pulpit, guitar in hand. She took a couple of deep breaths and began singing "Amazing Grace." When she finished, there was silence again.

Padre stepped to the pulpit and said, "Again, I thank you for coming. I hope all of you will introduce yourselves to Mr. Enrique Cordova. He's Rafael's brother, and he's here from Mexico City. Enrique, please stand, so the folks can see you. Refreshments will be served in the house. Please come through, meet Enrique, be served and come back outside. I think you can see that we cannot get everyone in the house at the same time. Now, please stand for the Benediction."

"Now may the grace of our Lord Jesus Christ, the love of God our Father and the communion of the Holy Spirit be with us all now and forever. Amen."

Enrique was the first to greet Padre. "Oh, Padre, I can't thank you enough. That was a wonderful service, from start to finish. Thank you for making a hard day a great day!"

Padre and Father Marquez were mobbed. They couldn't leave the pulpit area. When the line finally cleared them, they looked at each other. Father Marquez said to Padre, "Wow! What a homily!"

"Padre grinned and responded, "Wow, yourself! That was the prayer of prayers. I feel like I 've been to church."

"You have!" Father Marquez said, and laughed.

The two men shook hands and gave each other a big hug and separated. Padre looked at the crowd and decided he would be able to go to the house before long. He walked around on the property amid a stand of old live oak trees. He stopped under one especially beautiful tree and asked himself, "How can a place this beautiful be turned into something so evil?" He shook his head and moved on.

He heard the shrill cry once again. The peacocks were walking around the corner of the house. Padre stared at them for the longest time, then smiled and said, "Thank you. Thank you, peacocks. Thank you very much."

All of a sudden, he felt someone tap on his shoulder. He turned around quickly and saw Jose and Maria grinning at him.

"Oh, Padre, Maria said, "You said just exactly what I so needed to hear. I have really been struggling with my feelings about the Diablos, especially Diablo Guero. You were so good! I understood every word. You preach so everybody can understand."

"Well, thank you Maria. You are very kind."

"You want me to tell you what you said?"

"Maria, I said a lot. Are you sure you want to try this?"

"Oh, yes. I can tell you what you said easily."

"Okay. Go ahead."

"You told us, 'Don't be bitter! Be better!' True?"

"True." Padre paused for a moment, scratched his head, and said, "Maria, have you ever thought about being a preacher?"

"No!" she said emphatically.

"Why not?"

"Because, in my church, I'd have to be a nun," and looking adoringly at Jose, she said, "I don't want any part of that!"

"I understand. Believe me, I understand," Padre concluded.

"Padre, we never talked about where we were going to have our wedding."

"No, we didn't. I just figured that you hadn't found a place yet."

"We hadn't, but we have now."

"Oh? Where?"

"Here, at La Paloma. Outside, with the reception inside and on the grounds. We asked Mr. Cordova and he said yes. He said that he thought our wedding would be a perfect way to give La Paloma a new beginning."

"Then La Paloma it is!" Padre agreed.

"We have to go now," Maria said. "We've got a wedding to plan."

The three exchanged hugs, and Padre walked on toward the house.

Chapter Fifty Three

When Padre could see that the crowd had been through the serving line, he made his way up to the house. He couldn't shake the notion that he was about to see again the only part of the property he had ever seen before.

He walked through the entry hall and found himself immediately in the large family room. He stood and looked around the room. His heart began to beat faster. His breathing rate increased. His mind was spinning. He closed his eyes. He could visualize Diablo Guero holding court and loving every minute of it. Padre remembered how proud Diablo Guero was with his creation of "Monday Night Baseball." His mind flashed to Angel, who, according to Angel, would have no trouble hitting Mike "right between the eyes." He began to feel a tightness in his chest. Then he remembered the worst moment of all. He closed his eyes again and he could see Diego and Carlos walking gingerly into the big room carrying Raul's head on a large metal serving tray. A hard chill went up his spine. He began to cry. He walked out of the large family room and started down the bedroom wing of the house.

The doors all looked the same to him. He tried the first one he came to. He shuddered as he opened the door. It was his room. He only lived in it fewer than twenty four hours, but, as he looked at it, he felt like he was returning to some place that had been his home for years. The windows, the small bathroom, everything looked as he remembered it.

He closed his eyes again. He was looking at the rattlesnake that was the center piece of his horrible nightmare. He could hear Mike calling out for help. "Grandpa, Grandpa, is that you? Grandpa, I'm hurt! I can't move! Help me!" His tears began flowing again.

He remembered the look in Maria's eyes when he nodded in assent that he would help her. How, he thought, was I going to help her? I couldn't help myself. I guess the only thing that makes any sense at all is that I just couldn't take her hope away from her. Thank you, Lord. Thank you for answering our prayers.

He was standing in the middle of the bedroom when he began to tremble. His face felt flush, and his breathing was getting rapid and shallow. Maybe this is a mistake. Maybe I should never have entered this house again. He began to sob. He couldn't control it.

Suddenly, he felt a hand on his left shoulder. Then he felt an arm moving around his shoulders. He looked over his left shoulder. Juan was standing next to him. Padre looked at him through his tears, but he couldn't speak.

Juan patted him lightly on the shoulder. "It will get better, my friend. I know. The preacher said it would."

"You were listening?" Padre managed to say.

"I was. To every word! Come on, Padre, let's go home."

Chapter Fifty Four

The Brass Quintet of the Del Rio High School Ram Band played a medley of patriotic songs as the Paul Poag Auditorium filled. Padre, Midge, Dennis, Marilyn and Mike sat on the front row.

When the appointed time of 7:00 p.m. arrived, Mayor Julian Aleman stepped up to the lectern on the large stage. He surveyed the crowd and pointed to a few vacant seats left down toward the front. The ushers caught his signal and escorted several more family groups to still available seats. When they were seated, Mayor Aleman spread his open hands, indicating that there were no more available seats. The people who were still coming in began to spread out around the walls.

"Welcome," Mayor Aleman said, flashing a big smile. "We are so glad to see you this evening. I want you to know that you are in for a special evening as we honor a common man of uncommon courage."

The people applauded. "But I want first to express our thanks to the Brass Quintet from Del Rio High School."

There was more applause. "Let me assure those of you who have just arrived that we will hear more from them before the evening is over. Before I let them take a break, however, I am going to ask them to play our National Anthem. Then The Rev. Ramon Sanchez will give our Invocation."

Everyone rose on the first note and remained standing for the Invocation. Ramon stepped to the microphone and offered the prayer.

"Our Father, we are here this evening as a thankful and joyful people. We thank you for every expression of your grace, mercy and peace. We thank you that our friend Padre survived his ordeal at the hands of the Diablos. We thank you for giving him the plan and the courage to save his life and Mike's. We thank you for Marilyn's incredible courage and determination. We also thank you that Padre was able to disrupt the shipment of illegal drugs and, ultimately, destroy the Diablos. Bless us now, we pray, that we may draw from their examples and increase in our own willingness to trust you completely and serve you faithfully. We offer this prayer in the name of our Lord and Savior, Jesus Christ. Amen."

The mayor waited patiently until everyone was seated and the Brass Quintet had dispersed. He then got the twinkle in his eye that was his trademark and said, "Now, we have some presentations to make. I want first to call on Officer Steve Collier of the Del Rio Police Department."

Steve was seated on the second row next to a wall. He stepped forward and made his way up onto the stage. He stepped to the microphone and said, "Something old, something new…and stopped. He put his hand up to his right ear and said, "Come on, help me.'

The audience immediately responded in chorus with "something borrowed, something blue."

Steve smiled and applauded the audience. "Very good! Thank you! This evening we're only going to do the first two. It is my great pleasure to do the first of the two. Padre, I know you're not quite up to full speed health wise, but, one of these days, you're going to want to play golf again. And you're going to remember that your clubs were in the back of your Denali when you decided to take on "Padre Grande" single-handedly. You may already be wondering what ever happened to them. If you will join me on stage, I have a bit of a surprise for you."

Padre stood up, looked puzzled, and walked up on the stage. Steve shook his hand vigorously and said, "Just stay where you are."

Steve walked off stage and returned immediately carrying Padre's golf bag with all his clubs. Padre's eyes got big and his mouth flew open.

Steve handed Padre the bag of clubs. Padre looked at them long and hard, making sure every club was present and in its place, and said, "I have to admit. I thought I'd never see these again. Steve, thank you so much for caring for my clubs and bringing them back to me. This is very special."

"I have an offer to make to you."

"Oh?"

"Yes, I'll be your caddy for your first round."

"Well, Steve, that's a very generous offer, but I don't normally play with a caddy. I wouldn't know what to do with a caddy if I had one."

"Oh, that's okay. Don't worry about it. I don't know how to caddy anyway."

The audience was in stitches.

Padre shook hands with Steve and gave him a big hug, and Steve exited to his seat.

Padre was left standing alone with his golf bag and clubs. The mayor soon came to his rescue and said, "Padre, I'm glad to see that you have your clubs back, but you still have a problem. You don't have a good way to transport them to golf course. If you think you're going to put them in your old Denali, you need to think again. We had to remove your Denali from the wreck site. It really didn't add much to the beauty of 'Padre Grande.' We struggled with what to do with it. We emailed some pictures of it to a body shop here in town, thinking they might be able to repair it. But they emailed us back and said they didn't do 'reinventions.' So that idea didn't work. We then thought the military might be able to use it. So we asked the folks out at Laughlin. They told us to contact the Navy, but they said they didn't use anchors. Well, the Navy wasn't interested either, so we had to come up with another plan. Here, hold these keys for me, please?" Mayor Aleman said as he fumbled around in his coat pockets.

Padre obeyed. He took the keys and held them like they were the family jewels. He then tried to hand them back to Mayor Aleman.

"I don't want those keys," he said. "I don't have any use for them, but you do. They are to your new 2015 Acadia Denali, a gift from the people of Acuna, Del Rio and Val Verde County."

Padre was speechless. But the audience wasn't. They clapped and roared their approval.

Padre handed his bag of clubs off to Mayor Aleman, who gave them to a member of the Brass Quintet who took them off stage. Padre gave Mayor a handshake and hug.

Padre stepped to the microphone and said, "Thank you, Mayor Aleman. My friends, I thank you for being here this evening. Thank you for your wonderful kindness and generosity. I am overwhelmed! In fact, I stand before you this evening as a very grateful and humble man. I owe so many so much. Most of all I am grateful to the God and Father of our Lord Jesus Christ. I am grateful to him beyond measure for answering my prayer with a plan that he also made work. I was granted the gift of living out a miracle. I thank him for saving my life! I am grateful for His making it possible for Marilyn to get to Roosevelt Little League Park in time to save Mike. That's another miracle.

I'm sure you all are well aware of her life saving tackle. But you may not be aware that she has received a phone call from Jerry Johnson, asking her if she'd be interested in playing linebacker for the Dallas Cowboys. Our family is pleased that she has chosen to decline that offer."

The audience laughed and applauded Marilyn with a standing ovation.

"I would be remiss if I did not express our family's appreciation also to Officer Miguel Garcia of the Del Rio Police Department. God used Miguel to make sure Marilyn got to the ball park on time. Is Miguel here?"

Miguel was seated well toward the rear of the theatre. He rose, blushed, and smiled broadly at Padre. The crowd responded with a big round of applause.

"By the way, Miguel, from what Marilyn has told me about her trip from the hospital to Roosevelt, I have decided that if you get tired of being a police officer, you have a bright future in NASCAR." The crowd roared.

"I am also very grateful to the wonderful staff of the Val Verde Regional Medical Center and Hospital CEO Bob Garfield, in particular. Bob not only oversees a competent and caring staff, he also exercised great flexibility and administrative skill in aiding our dear friend Texas Ranger Juan Garza in the stopping of another attempt on my life while I was in the hospital."

The audience gasped. They had heard nothing about the attempt the Diablos made to kill Padre in the hospital.

"Bob and Juan, will you please stand so we may thank you?"

Bob and Juan stood and received a huge ovation. Before Juan sat down, he smiled at Padre and winked.

"Juan also initiated and coordinated an attack with the Mexican Army on the Diablos at their compound at the La Paloma Ranch, south and east of Acuna. We are not only glad that the Diablos have been taken out of business, we are also very proud of our working relationship with the Mexican government. Friends, you know as well as I, that the border is not about we and they. It's about our working together as one. Juan, thank you again."

More applause followed.

"Last, but certainly not least, I want to thank all of you who prayed for my safety and recovery. I feel so blessed to count you as my friends. Thank you all very much for everything, but especially for being you,"

Padre slowed down just enough to shake Mayor Aleman's hand one more time. He walked off the stage to a standing ovation.

Mayor Aleman stepped to the lectern once more and said, "Padre, thank you for being you."

When Padre was seated, Mayor Aleman said, "We wrestled long and hard with the matter of a speaker for this very special occasion. We first thought we would ask the governor, but then we said to ourselves, 'We can do better than that.' Then we thought we might ask a congressman or a senator, but we said to ourselves 'We can do better than that.' Then we thought we might just shoot the works and invite the President of the United States, but, again, we said to ourselves, 'We can do better than that.' So we decided that we would go really first class. And, we have invited our own Mike Duncan to be our guest speaker."

The crowd roared.

Mike stood up, winked at Padre, and made his way to the lectern. He cleared his throat a couple of times and said, "Thank you, Mayor Aleman."

He arranged the few notes he had and then said, "I want first to give full credit to my speech consultant, my Mom, Marilyn Duncan."

The audience jumped to their feet again and exploded with applause. Someone in the back yelled "Marilyn for President!" The standing ovation took a full two minutes.

Mike waited patiently until the audience settled down in their seats. Then he began, "My name is Mike Duncan, and the title of my speech is 'What Is a Hero?'

I am twelve years old. I play football, basketball and baseball at my school. I love sports, and I have great respect for everyone who plays sports. But my heroes are not athletes, amateur or professional.

The reason athletes are not my heroes is that I believe athletes are just people who have special talents, just like the guys who play in the Brass Quintet have special talents. There are lots of special talents spread across this audience here this evening. I'm sorry, if you expect me to think you're my hero just because you have a special talent. I don't.

Besides, if I did want athletes to be my heroes, how would I go about picking the one or ones who would be heroes to me? And how often would I have to change them?

Would I pick the hero who quarterbacked the winning Super Bowl team, or the pitcher who won the 7th game of the World Series, or the one who just got the biggest signing bonus or just signed the biggest contract of all time, or the one who finally passed a drug test?

I'd be really confused. I could end up with more heroes than I'd know what to do with.

No, my heroes are not athletes. My hero is not an athlete. He does play golf, but he has a terrible slice."

The audience roared with laughter.

"But I don't care, Mike continued. " Because he is still my number one, all-world hero. My hero is my grandpa. My hero is the Rev. Earl Thomas "Padre" Reynolds. Why is he my hero? Because I think he is the bravest man in the world! Thank you."

The audience rose again with still another standing ovation. One wag said, as he got up out of his seat again, "Honey, does it feel to you like we're spending about as much time standing here as sitting?"

"Hush, Leonard!" his wife said. And he did.

When Mike returned to his seat, Padre welcomed him with a prolonged hug.

"Thank you, Mike," Mayor Aleman said. "Please know that none of those people I mentioned as possible speakers could have done anywhere near as good a job as you did."

When the audience settled down again, Mayor Aleman said, "Again, I thank you for coming. We are going to close as we began. The Brass Quintet is going to play "America the Beautiful" for us. They have asked me to ask you to let them play it once alone and then join them for a second playing. Thank you and good night."

The Brass Quintet took their places again. The music filled the huge theatre.

Chapter Fifty Five

"My sister Consuela is going to be my maid of honor, and the bridesmaids are going to be my cousins Esperanza, Lucinda and Angelina, and Manuel Garcia is going to be Jose's best man, and Lemuel Zuniga, Carlos Sanchez and Miguel Marquez, Jose's army buddies, are going to be the groomsmen, and my little niece, Rosalinda, is going to be the flower girl, and Miranda is going to sing twice, and the bridesmaids are going to wear light green dresses, and the men are going to wear white tuxedos with green ties, and Juan Delgado is going to video everything, and the reception is going to be in the house, and…

"Whoa… Maria!" Padre said. "I think I've got the picture. It'll be a lovely wedding."

"Oh, Padre, it's just going to be perfect!"

Jose said, "I would just as soon have us married right here in your living room."

"Well, now, Jose," Padre said, "Men and women tend to take different views on weddings."

"I guess."

"By the way, where are you planning to go on your honeymoon?"

Maria stiffened. Her face got red. She gritted her teeth. "He won't tell me!"

Padre smiled and said, "He won't even give you a little hint?"

"Well, maybe a little one," Maria said and giggled. "All he will say is 'Bring your bikini.'"

Chapter Fifty Six

Padre took his place between two large oak trees, looked out on the smiling, expectant assembly of family and friends, and said, "Dearly, beloved, we are assembled here in the presence of God, to join Jose and Maria in holy marriage…"

Postscript: In case you are wondering whatever happened to Eduardo, the man who was to deliver the money to Diego, please be advised that he is no longer waiting. The latest rumor, uncon-firmed, of course, suggests that he is living a very comfortable life in retirement in a remote area of Argentina, courtesy of the Rev. Earl Thomas "Padre" Reynolds.

Acknowledgments

Special thanks are in order for my son Steve of Fredericksburg, Texas. Steve introduced me to Mr. Kurt Lemp of Del Rio, Texas. Kurt made it possible for me to do extensive interviews with officers of the Del Rio Police Department and The Customs Border Protection officers serving at the International Crossing at Del Rio. The information these gentlemen gave me made the story possible and gave it credibility. Thank all of you very much.

I am also indebted to my longtime friend Euardo Zuniga, whose idea it was to name our cartel leader Diablo Guero (white devil). Thank you, Ed.

I would be remiss if I did not acknowledge the tremendous help of my wife Shirley. She brought her considerable computer skills and editorial insights to bear in her always patient and practical demeanor. Thanks, Sweetheart.

Most of all, I want to thank God. He is the source of all good inspiration. He came through for me again in all those moments when I found myself short on ideas and the will to pursue the project to completion.